Home Sweet Home

& Other Dangerous Places

Home Sweet Home

& Other Dangerous Places

By Julie Failla Earhart

A Toots Publication
ISBN 978-0-6151-6516-5
October 2007

All of the stories included in this manuscript are the work of fiction. Names, characters, places, and incidents either are the product of the author's imagination or are used fictitiously, and any resemblance to actual persons, living or dead, business establishments, events or locales is entirely coincidental.

For Momma and Daddy.
For believing even when they didn't understand
and
for always providing a safe home.

Contents

Acknowledgments

Thanks to my co-hort in life, John Ellis, for his unwavering support. Thanks to Momma and Daddy for their unconditional love and support, no matter what I do. Thanks to Steve McAllister who has done the hard part of formatting this manuscript and for his dear friendship. Also a great big thank you for the cover picture. Thanks to the Feasting Foxes—Lisa Ebert, Mike McGuire, Lisa Miller, Denise Mussman, Arnold Traubitz, and the late Travis Black—and my fellow scribblers in the University of Missouri-St. Louis' MFA program between 1996 and 2000 for their many comments and critiques on almost all of these stories in one shape or another. Thanks to the in professors at UM-St. Louis English Department. Your gentle sculpting is deeply appreciated. Most important, thanks to David Carkeet, novelist and professor, without whom an MFA program at UMSL would not exist. You saw my potential and admitted me to the program. I love your work and will always be a fan!

Home Sweet Home

Jillian

Jillian fumbled through the assortment of currency in her hands. "I'm sorry. How much did you say?"

"Twenty-five dollars." The cab driver began drumming his fingers on the steering wheel in-sync with the banjo music playing on the radio.

Jillian's red-gold hair covered her face as she picked out two tens and five ones and an additional two dollar tip. Shaking her hair out of the way, she stuck a trembling hand through the heavy plastic-coated partition. "How much to wait until I get inside and turn on a light?"

The cab driver turned as fully toward the backseat as his big belly allowed and raised his thick, black eyebrows.

Jillian repeated the question.

The cab driver shrugged. "I dunno. Two dollars, I guess."

"I'll give you five if you wait until I walk through the house and blink the lights twice."

The cab driver looked over the young woman. She had deep, dark circles under her jade green eyes, a pasty white face, and a thick, if somewhat masculine, physique. She was well dressed but her hair was slicked down on her head as if hadn't been washed in several days. He turned back toward the front seat while his black eyes wandered over the neatly manicured lawns, the gingerbread cottages and the high-priced vehicles sitting in most of the driveways. "This is a nice neighborhood."

"Yes. Yes. It is. Very nice. And safe. Very safe." She pushed the crisp five through the plastic-glass barrier. "Remember. Twice. I'll blink them twice. If I haven't in, say, three minutes, call the police."

The cab driver swiveled in his seat. "The police? Hey, now, I don't want to get involved in any fight with your husband or nothing."

"I don't have a husband." Jillian flinched at involuntarily giving out that piece of information. She hadn't even gotten into the house yet and she had already broken her new vow. "You won't get involved in anything; I promise. If you have to call the cops, make the call, then leave. That's all you have to do."

"I don't know," he said slowly.

Jillian rummaged through the money in her purse again, pulled out a twenty and shoved it toward the square hole. "Here. Does this help?"

The cab driver took the crumpled bill. "Yeah, I guess, but only three minutes, then I'm outta here."

Jillian picked up her keys and found the one to the front door. She looked out the rear seat window at her three-bedroom ranch home. The bit of light emanating from the yellowish street lamp did little to pierce the darkness of her front porch. Did the light burn out, she wondered, or was it turned off on purpose? As she opened the car door a blast of frigid wind hurtled itself against her. Who said it never gets cold in St. Louis?

"The weatherman said we're going to have a ice storm Wednesday night," the cab driver said.

Jillian turned and looked at him. "I'm sorry. I didn't realize that I was talking out loud."

The cab driver shrugged.

"Wednesday, huh?"

"That's what he said. Sure feels like it could."

Jillian reached beside her for her overnight bag and stepped into another whip of wind. She poked her head back in. "Three minutes, okay? You promised," and slammed the door without waiting for the cab driver to reply.

On unsteady legs, Jillian walked as fast as she could up the sidewalk while juggling the keys, her purse and her bag, then climbed the two steps to the porch. A quick glance told her everything was in its place. She opened the door and stepped inside, shutting and locking the door and flipping on the light with one fluid motion. With her back to the door, she faced the rectangular-shaped living/dining room. Magazines and crossword puzzle books were piled high on the coffee table and stacked high near the right end of the brown plaid sofa. Here, too, everything was in its place. No fuss, no muss.

She dropped her bags on the area rug. Taking a deep breath, she walked the length of the room to the kitchen. The soft whir of the ceiling fan stirred as she turned on the light. The rum, tequila, Crown Royal, and Schnapps bottles were sitting on the counter. The door above the refrigerator hung open. Other than the bottles, which were lined neatly in a row the way she left them, all was in order. Crossing the room, she shut the cabinet door and double-checked the locked doors to the basement and the back yard.

For the first time since she bought the house seven years earlier, Jillian was grateful that she had passed on the six-bedroom, two-story place over on Waterloo. She would never be able to handle returning to a place that large. Not after…not after…that phone call.

She made her way down the narrow hallway to the first bedroom, the one where she did her ironing and made quilts that she sold at local craft fairs. She winced as the harsh light of a 100-watt bulb flared at her. Everything was straight. She blinked the lights twice and listened as the cab driver gunned the engine and pulled away. Slumping against the doorjamb of the room, Jillian didn't know if she had the energy to make her way to her bedroom, the last room at the end of the hallway.

The second bedroom was a guestroom or, more precisely, her parents' room when they came to visit from Florida. Jillian took a quick peep. The only time she went into that room was to air it out and make the bed the day before a planned parental visit. Taking a deep breath, she straightened and slowly walked the rest of the way down the hall, using the wall to keep her balance.

Jillian knew what she'd find when she would enter. There hadn't been a lot of blood. She hadn't even realized she'd been bleeding until she noticed that a corner of the blue-striped flannel sheet was wet. There was a spot on the underside of the navy comforter where the blood had soaked into its downy fibers. Was that before or after Raymond had come to get her? She shook her head, trying to clear away the blurry images. Her eyes searched the room. The top bureau drawer had been left open. The pillowcase, partially filled with costume jewelry, a bottle of vodka and the bag that she had claimed was her purse, was on the floor. The doors of her jewelry case were wide open.

5

When she reached the end of the hallway, she stopped at the doorway of her bedroom. The door was closed. Something she never did. Not even at night. Not even when Raymond slept over. Did he close it? Jillian rubbed her arms, more to steady her nerves than to warm herself in the cold house. Okay, okay, you can do it, she thought. You can go in there. There's nothing to be afraid of. Maybe you should have let Raymond come with you. Or Anita. Or maybe hired a security guard for the night. No one is hiding in there. No one can see you. Still, she stood, rooted to the hardwood floor, unable to open the door.

Raymond

My assistant, Marge, pulled me out of a meeting with the CFO when Jillian called. We were discussing next year's marketing budget. She said Jillian was hysterical, and she was right. Jillian kept repeating three sentences, "Come over. Come over now. It's an emergency." I couldn't get anything else out of her. I had no choice but to go.

It takes me about fifteen minutes to get from my office at Delany & Associates downtown to her house over on Jefferson. I leaped up the front steps, scooped up the pillowcase that was lying outside the screen door and rushed right in. Now that I think back on it, I remember it was heavy and something jingled and a thought flitted across my mind that this was weird.

Then nothing. Everything seemed to be okay. I called her name; she didn't answer. I guess I had expected the house to be on fire, a burglar to be ransacking the place or standing over her unconscious and bleeding body, or something obvious, but everything was in its place. Or so it was in the living room.

At first, I thought this was a trick, perhaps she had taken the day off from her job as a real estate agent and wanted to spend the rest of the day in bed. The pillowcase I had picked up outside the front door and now clutched in my right hand was throwing me off. I looked at my watch; it was 9:05. She had done this a few times in the two years we've been together. She had never used an 'emergency' as a stunt before. But with everything in its place and no Jillian, I wasn't so sure.

My initial reaction was to be pissed. She knew how important the meeting with Don Delany, Sr., was and how much my career as the marketing director at one of St. Louis' most prestigious advertising firms depended on it. I couldn't lose this job; I'm too damned old to be the new kid on the block anymore. So I started down the hallway, determined to give her a sound tongue-lashing. In my subconscious, I could see her sitting cross-legged on the bed in her red silk teddy and that come hither look in her eyes and those legs that went on forever. How dare she pull this today! When I reached her bedroom, I was so pissed off I could have strangled her.

The minute I saw her, I knew something was terribly, terribly wrong. Jillian wasn't sitting on the bed; she was stretched out on the floor on her side as if she were trying to hide beneath the bed. And she was naked. With one of those lacy throw pillows clutched to her chest. Her eyes were wild and darting; she was scared shitless. The denuded pillow, a pink candle and the jar of moisturizer were on the unmade bed.

The pillowcase made a loud thunk when I dropped it on the floor. Jillian jumped and turned towards me. She grabbed me by pant's leg. "Get down. They can see you," she said in a voice that was a cross between a hissing noise and whisper with a bit of stammer thrown in.

I dropped down beside her. 'Who?'

She shook her head, red-gold flashing in all directions. "They said they were from the phone company and they could see everything I was doing. I wasn't supposed to call anyone or anything. They might come back."

I put my arm around her cold shoulders and tried to pull out the lace pillow, but she had a tight grip on it. I peered over her head. 'No one can see in,' I told her.

"Yes they can; they can see every move we're making."

I looked around the room and saw that her underwear drawer was open and that her jewelry case was empty. 'Who are "they?"'

Jillian

Jillian took a deep breath, holding it as she grabbed the brass doorknob to her bedroom and swung the heavy door back. She braced herself in case someone jumped out at her. Nothing. No one. There was no one in the house but her. Maybe I should get a dog, she thought. A big one. A Rottweiler or a German Shepherd or maybe a Doberman. She stood on the threshold for several minutes before turning on the light.

Her lungs forced her to take a breath. The light seemed bright. Had Raymond changed the light bulb? Why would he do that? The bed was still unmade, but the jar of moisturizer had been returned to its place on her night stand. The candles were gone: the pink one that had lain on the sheet and the blue one she had stuffed under the comforter right after ... right after...

She remembered handing that one to Raymond. I wonder what he did with it? The pillowcase was still lying on the floor but now the bag that she had claimed was her purse was beside it instead of inside it. Still, it was lighter than she remembered. Someone, Raymond probably, had removed the vodka bottle. The only thing left was a wad of costume jewelry, a bra and panties and eleven dollars---the only cash she'd had in the house. She had grabbed the jewelry and dropped it into the pillowcase, so it was probably hopelessly tangled.

Jillian walked over to the bureau and shut the top drawer. Bending over slightly, she pulled open the bottom drawer. She lifted her favorite purple cashmere sweater to see if the gun was still there. Right next to it were the bullets. She lifted the .38; it's heaviness felt good, then she loaded it and placed it next to her jewelry case. She used to be a good shot twenty, twenty-five years ago, when she was a teenager. Why didn't I keep this loaded, she wondered? Why didn't I hang up and grab the gun? I probably could have gotten it loaded before they got in. They wouldn't have known it wasn't loaded. But they said they had been in the house; they had watched me sleeping and knew where everything was.

With the .38 fully loaded and placed carefully on top of the bureau, Jillian slowly shut the doors of her jewelry case. Then she made the bed and sat down on the right side. She knew she should strip it and soak the sheets, but not tonight. She was too tired; too scared. She usually slept on the left, but she wasn't ready to actually place her body on that side. I'll sleep on the sofa tonight, she thought. Or maybe forever.

Raymond

She said she didn't know who 'they' were. There was only one person on the line, but 'they' were from the phone company. I asked her if she recognized the voice, but she shook her head no. I asked her if anybody had come in the house but she stared at the floor like she couldn't hear me. Then I wondered if she'd been raped. There had been a series of rapes in other parts of St. Louis over the past few years. The newspapers had dubbed the guy 'The Southside Rapist,' but the cops had finally caught him and he was doing life in prison, I think, somewhere.

I tried to stand up but she grabbed my arm and pulled me back so hard that I almost lost my balance. She wouldn't let go; her grip was so powerful that I have bruises from her fingers on my arm. And that was through my shirt sleeves, my suit jacket and my overcoat. That was something; she may have a square kinda build, but she is dainty and feminine. She can't even lift a ten pound bowling ball or a heavy log for the fireplace.

Anyway, I caught myself with my free hand and tried to get her to talk to me. All she would do was stare at the floor. I knelt beside her and pried, yes, pried, her fingers off my arm, then wrapped my arms around her as best I could. I still had my overcoat on and she still had the lace pillow clutched to her chest. That gave me the chance to look around.

The first thing I saw was the pink candle and the jar of moisturizer on the bed. She liked to rub that stuff on her feet; said it made them feel better after a day in nylons and high heels. The candle was a mystery. The wick had been burned, but she had burned all the wicks in all the candles in the house. Said it was bad luck if they were left unlit. Her pajamas were hung on the post of the wrought iron bedpost—the one we bought at a yard sale last year on that impromptu antique-shopping trip to Hannibal. She liked to sleep naked; said she couldn't ever remember wearing a nightgown or pajamas but was certain that she had when she had been a kid. Her parents were strict Catholics and conservative.

Her favorite blanket---the one that had been her grandmother's---was heaped on my side of the bed. I sleep over most weekends, but during the week, I hate to fight the traffic; I own a loft next door to my office building on Washington Ave. I know, I know. It's only fifteen minutes, but I despise sitting on Highway 40 and barely moving.

Then I saw that her top bureau drawer was open and that the doors to her jewelry case were open. The bottom drawer of her jewelry case was also open, but the top drawer was shut. I wondered about the diamond and ruby ring that had been her mother's. She loved that ring and it was quite valuable. Maybe somebody had seen her wear it when we went see *La travita* at the Rep last week and decided…no, those types of people don't break into houses on the Southside. I thought it was kind of strange that the top drawer to her jewelry case was closed when everything else was open, but then again, the whole thing seemed strange.

I didn't notice the blood. Not at first. I was stroking her hair and rocking her back and forth, like you do to comfort a kid. It was when I leaned over to kiss her head that I noticed the blood. There wasn't a lot, but, my God, it was blood. Blood! I let her go and looked over her body. I couldn't see that she had been cut or punched on anything. I jumped up, dragging her with me. She tried to sink back down to the floor, but I steered her toward the bed. I tried to get her to sit on it, but she started screaming 'they can see me,' so I let her back down to the floor, 'We're going to the hospital,' I told her. As I went into the bathroom to get her robe, she yelled, "No cops. We can't call the police. They might come back."

That scared me even more.

Jillian

She fingered the blinds that covered the plate glass window. Gently, she lifted two apart and placed her face against the cold plastic blinds. The front porch light bulb was burned out so she could barely see past empty clay flower box that sat on the ledge. I'll change it tomorrow, she thought.

Jillian sneezed as she let go of the blinds. I need to get a rag and…

She jumped when the phone rang. She watched it ring three more times before running over to the bureau and picking up the gun. Without removing the gun from its holster, she unsnapped the strap that held it firmly in its leather home. The barrel was pointed at the doorway. The recorder would pick up on the tenth ring. She listened to the sound of her own voice from the living room.

"Jill, you there, honey? It's me. Pick up if you're there."

Jillian breathed a sigh of relief. It was Raymond.

"Jillian, honey? Are you there?"

She grabbed the bedside phone and placed a breathless "Hello" into the receiver.

"What's wrong? Are you all right? What…"

"I'm okay; I wasn't expecting the phone to ring and it scared me. I'm okay, really."

"How long have you been there?"

Jillian was silent.

"Do you want me to come over?"

"No." She paused. "Yes. No." She sat down on bed. "Yes. No, no. I need to do this."

"That doesn't mean you have to spend your first night out of the hospital alone. Why don't you call Anita?"

Anita was Jillian's roommate in college and they were still best friends.

"No, I don't think so. It's not that I don't appreciate your concern, Raymond, it's that, well, you know."

Raymond's husky voice, which normally sent shivers up her spine, softened. "Why don't you let me stay with you tonight? You can get used to being there by yourself tomorrow during the day."

"What happened to me happened during the day."

"I know that." Jillian heard the exasperation in his voice. "Wouldn't it be easier if..." Raymond sighed on his end of the phone. "I know but I don't feel right about it."

"If it makes you feel any better, I loaded the gun and put it next to the bed." As she made a mental note to put the gun on her bedside table, Jillian heard the sharp intake of Raymond's breath.

"You did what?"

"I loaded the gun; I promise I'll be careful. Besides, with the sleeping pills Dr. Ferrera gave me, I'll probably be out like a light."

"You gotta be careful with those too."

"Yes, Raymond. I know that." She pretended to yawn. "I'm tired. I'm gonna hang up now."

"Okay. Call me if you need anything or get scared or anything."

Jillian smiled into the phone. He was such a worrywart.

"I love you. Bye."

She started at his announcement. He had never said that before. She continued to stare at the phone as the dial tone began to hum. Why did he have to say that now, tonight of all nights?

Raymond

After I wrestled the lace pillow away from her, lifted her off the floor and got her into her robe, I tried to sit her down on the bed again. She jerked away from me, crying and screaming 'they can see me' and ran over to cower in the corner next to the bookcase.

'Okay,' I told her and stepped back. 'We're going to the hospital. Tell me what you need and I'll get it.'

Then as if a switch had been flipped, she stopped and stared straight at me like nothing had happened. Her eyes were still lifeless, but, I don't know. There was this intense sanity about her. Not that I'm saying she was insane or anything, but at that moment, the controlled, together, determined woman I knew and loved was back. I still didn't know what happened and, to be honest, I was afraid to ask. I waited for her to make the next move.

We must have stood there for a minute or two, then she calmly walked over to the bed and reached beneath the blanket. 'Here,' she said, 'this is what happened,' and held out her hand.

I stuck out my hand, but my eyes never left her face, watching for any sign of impending hysteria. She placed something cold and kind of slimy in my hand and took a step back. I looked down to see a blue candle, one of those with the swirl pattern, that had been broken in two but still connected by its wick and it was covered with some kind of film. The wick was a dark red, like dried blood. I looked at her for some answers. Her jaw was set and she stared at my hand. 'This is what happened,' she said.

'I don't understand,' I said to her.

'They made me do it,' she said. 'They said they'd come into the house and hurt me if I didn't.'

'Are you hurt anywhere,' I asked her, but she didn't answer. I asked who, and what, and how, while she stared at my hand. 'But the blood...'

I'm not bleeding.' She said it in her *Raymond, you can be so stupid sometimes* voice.

'There's blood on the bed,' I said and pointed. She walked over, slowly, and touched the spots.

'Wow, this is soaked,' she said. 'I need to put these in the laundry before we go.'

I opened my mouth to say something, but I didn't have time. Jillian opened her robe and looked down at her body. 'I don't think I'm bleeding anymore.' She took the robe off, turned and tried to look at her body over her shoulder. 'I don't see anything; do you see anything?'

I didn't see any blood or marks of any kind, which made frightened me more. Where did it come from? What happened to her? Finally, I walked over and put my arms around her, but she was stiff as a board. I wondered if I should call an ambulance or the police, but I wasn't sure what to do. We must have stood like that for two or three minutes, but the tension never left her body. 'Let's go to the hospital and get you checked out,' I whispered in her ear.

She nodded and began to push me away. 'I have to get ready first,' she said.

I told her that she shouldn't shower or anything, in case the doctor wanted to examine her. She said she wasn't going anywhere naked and headed for the bathroom.'I don't think that's a good idea,' I said to her retreating back.

The water in the shower began to run. Then I realized I was still holding the blue candle. I didn't know what to do with it so I threw it in the trash.

While she was showering, I walked through the house. Everything looked okay. I mean there weren't any smashed-in doors or broken windows and the door to the basement was still locked. I was on my way out of the kitchen when I noticed the bottles of alcohol neatly lined up on the counter. The vodka bottle was missing. That was another weird thing. Jillian doesn't drink. Hasn't had a drink in the two years I've known her and I understand it's been at least ten since she quit. I looked at 'em all neatly lined up there---the rum, tequila, Crown Royal, and Schnapps---like little wooden soldiers. I wish I could remember everything that was going through my head, but I don't. All I can remember thinking is that there wasn't any bourbon. Bourbon was Jillian's choice of booze when she drank. At least that's what she had told me.

I heard her turn the shower off so I poked my head inside the bathroom. I couldn't really see her though the steam. I asked her if she was ready. She said she had to put her makeup on.

I scratched my head at that one. Why would she need to put makeup on to go to the hospital? I asked her if she wanted me to pack her an overnight bag, but she brushed by me and said she really didn't know why we had to go in the first place, that she would be okay, and that she wasn't staying overnight. What was done, was done and couldn't be undone.

Jillian

Could he really be in love with me, she wondered. Jillian craved passion and romance. Especially with her thirty-fifth birthday coming next year. She was way behind schedule for passion, romance, adventure and children. Raymond wasn't all that passionate, after the first six months of their affair anyway. He definitely wasn't romantic. She'd never gotten flowers on her birthday or candy on Valentine's Day, yet he said he loved her.

Jillian hung up the phone and wandered around the house, holstered gun in hand, careful to avoid too much movement in front of any window. They might be watching, she thought. The philodendron in the kitchen's bay window looked droopy, but it would have to wait until later.

She stretched out on the couch with the gun lying on her stomach, grabbed the remote from the coffee table and flicked through the channels. For the first time, she wished she had let Raymond persuade her into subscribing to cable, wished there were one of those stupid sitcoms airing that would help her not to think. She didn't want to think about what had happened. Let it go, she thought. It's done, it's over and there's nothing you can do about it.

Raymond

As soon as Jillian had finished her makeup and grabbed one of her crossword puzzle books, we drove over to Barnes Jewish Hospital. She insisted that I not let her out at the Emergency Room, but that I park in the lot and walk in. I wanted to disagree, but at the same time, I didn't want her going in there by herself.

When the nurse asked her the problem, she said, 'They made me do it. They said they'd come into the house and hurt me if I didn't.'

The nurse looked at her and then at me. I told her everything I knew at this point...finding her crying hysterically, the part about Jillian thinking somebody could see into the house and the blood. I left out the part about the candles and the moisturizer. I wasn't really sure about that, so I left it out.

It must have been close to noon by the time we finished signing in and sat down. Fortunately, the place wasn't busy. We had barely sat down and got our coats off when her name was called. I asked her if she wanted me to go with her and she shrugged. So I gathered up our stuff and followed her.

Dr. Sid Ferrera, MD

After looking at her chart, I expected to see a mad person when I walked in there. Jillian Peabody was sitting on the examining table as calm and rational as could be. I introduced myself and sat down on the stool.

She smiled and nodded.

I asked why she was here and she started straight ahead at the wall. There was a swarthy older man leaning against the wall on the far side of the room. I knew his name was Raymond Henson from the chart, but I wasn't clear as to their relationship. I asked who he was and they answered at the same time. She said, 'A friend.' He said, 'Her boyfriend.'

I had this funny feeling below the left side of my ribcage I always get when I know that everything isn't kosher. I asked Jillian if she wanted him to stay. She didn't react. Nothing. Like I hadn't asked her a question. Then he started to talk.

He told me what he knew, which I pretty much already knew from the notes Nurse Cohen had taken. As he repeated the whole scenario, she never moved. When he finished, she didn't move a muscle.

That's when I asked Mr. Henson to leave the room. I could tell he was going to balk by the way he shifted their jackets and her purse. I was polite, but firm. I told him I needed to examine Jillian alone.

After he left, I put my face level with Jillian's and looked straight into her eyes. Her pupils weren't dilated, so I ruled out drugs. She smelled a little like alcohol, but I didn't know what kind. I asked her if she hurt anywhere.

She looked down at her folded hands and said, 'My rectum hurts.'

That surprised me.

'They made me do it,' she said. 'They said they'd come into the house and hurt me if I didn't.'

Didn't do what?

'Everything they said.'

Who are they?

'I don't know. I only heard one voice. And a train. I heard a locomotive in the background.'

She was beginning to get a little agitated so I backed off. I asked her if it would be okay if I examined her. While I was getting her a hospital gown, I explained that I needed her vitals, that Nurse Cohen would take them, then stepped out of the room.

Raymond

I was waiting right outside the door when Dr. Ferrera came out and the nurse went in. He told me that she was suffering from Post Traumatic Stress Syndrome, that she was changing into a hospital gown and that he was going to examine her. He kept his head down, writing on the clipboard, like he didn't want to look at me. I asked him if Jillian was going to be okay, but he turned on his heel and went back into the room with her. Over his shoulder he told me to wait in the Waiting Room.

Dr. Sid Ferrera, MD

I gave Nurse Cohen few minutes to complete her task before I went back into the Examining Room. Her clothes were neatly draped on the back of the chair. She was lying flat on the table, staring at the ceiling.

I coughed lightly, not wanting to startle her. She didn't flinch a muscle or blink. I knew I was out of my league, that I would have to call in a psychiatrist, but it was my job to make sure that her body wasn't damaged.

'Your blood pressure, temperature, and pulse rate are all normal,' I told her. I had her do a few eye-hand coordinates. She did everything I asked of her without speaking. The movement of her extremities was normal. I didn't see any signs of abrasions on her face, necks, arms, and legs. When I asked her if she was hurting, she turned her head away from me and repeated 'my rectum' in a monotone voice.

I told her I needed to examine her and she slowly turned over, as if she was in some pain and raised her gown. As I pulled on latex gloves, I did a quick visual of her head, back, arms and legs. She looked to be the picture of health; her skin was a soft pink and supple. There were no abrasions on her buttocks.

She flinched when I touched her with the tips of my fingers. I started right at the tailbone and gently probed. 'Tell me when you feel pain,' I told her. She lifted her head and looked over her shoulder at me.

'Inside,' she said. 'It hurts inside.'

As easily as I could, I spread her buttocks. Around her anus was some dried blood and something else. It looked waxy and was a darker shade than blood. I could tell that at some point she had developed hemorrhoids because of the pockets of puffy flesh.

After I finished my visual, I told her that I would need to scrape some of the particles of the waxy substance for analysis. I told her that I wanted to feel around inside, to make sure everything was okay. Beneath my fingertips, I felt her tense.

She said that wasn't necessary; it was candle wax, some of the candle that she been forced to insert must have crumbled. I looked at Nurse Cohen and she looked at me.

'Candle wax?'

Nurse Cohen looked quickly down at the floor. We see a lot, and I mean a lot, of strange stuff here in ER, but candle wax?

I told her I needed to check for internal bleeding and that I would need to keep her overnight for observation to make sure that she didn't hemorrhage nor have any other injuries that hadn't surfaced yet. Given how tense she was and what I imagined might have happened, I thought it best to check via x-ray instead of a finger probe. I closed the gown and asked Jillian to sit up. Then I pulled the stool directly in front of her and asked her pointblank: 'Have you been sodomized?'

She nodded. 'They made me do it,' she said. 'They said they'd come into the house and hurt me if I didn't.'

'Did your friend do this to you?'

She shook her head no.

'Have you called the police?'

She shook her head no again.

'Do you want to file a report?'

Other than a downturn of her lips, she didn't respond. I'd ask the guy who brought her here. I had a sneaky feeling that they'd been experimenting sexually, but who am I to judge? Still, I needed to call in a psychiatrist and the police. I had never met Jillian Peabody until an hour earlier, but she wasn't responding normally.

I asked Nurse Cohen to get her set up with a room. I took her chart and went to the ER office. I had some phone calls to make.

Jillian

Jillian turned off the television and shifted to a more comfortable position on the couch, gun lying on the floor beside her. Her thoughts began to go back to that morning. Was it only yesterday? It seemed that her whole life had changed in the past forty-eight hours. Would she ever feel safe again? Could she ever sleep in her bedroom again? Would she ever be able to answer the phone again?

She knew she could call her parents. They hadn't heard from her in three days. That wasn't unusual since they'd retired to Florida ten years ago. Her mom usually called on late Sunday mornings, right after they got home from the 10 a.m. mass at St. Brendan's.

Jillian stared up at the ceiling, let the quiet engulf her. As if detached from her body and mind, she watched a rerun of Monday morning.

Dr. Sid Ferrera, MD

First I called the Third Precinct and talked with a Detective Quinlan Moynihan. He said that he'd drop by and see what was up, although he agreed that it sounded like some type of sexual oddity they were trying; he'd heard, and seen, more perverse. It was 'they' that Jillian kept referring to that bothered him. There hadn't been any burglaries nor rapes reported in the St. Louis Hills neighborhood.

Then I called Lily Perry, a psychotherapist who had a practice here at Barnes. She, too, agreed with my diagnosis, but her concern was Jillian's lack of reaction. She said she would drop by Jillian's room after her group session this evening for a little chat. I went out and explained to

Mr. Henson that I was going to keep Ms. Peabody overnight for observation. I knew that it was Moynihan's job to question Henson, but I couldn't help myself.

I bluntly asked him what they had been doing. He repeated the exact same story he had told earlier, so I left it at that. I didn't tell him about the chats I had had with Moynihan and Lily. He wasn't her husband or guardian. Then I went back into ER Room 7 and told Jillian that I wanted to take a few x-rays and that I wanted to keep her overnight, to make sure there was no more hemorrhaging. I also told her that Lily would be dropping by to see her and that we'd talk again after the x-rays came back.

Raymond

The nurses took Jillian off to get her x-rays and said that I could go on up Room 447 and wait.

Thankfully, the other bed was empty. I don't think she needed a lot of other people around right now. It was like she was in some sort of fog or that her mind shut down.

I waited in her room for about an hour before a nurse wheeled her in. I made a small fuss over her, hoping that would make her feel a little better. I told her how glad I was that they had finished and how happy I was to see her and all that kind of stuff. She climbed dutifully into bed.

She lay there, on her side, staring at the wall. Dr. Ferrera came in about three and checked on her. There were no internal damages that he could see, but he still wanted to keep her overnight, in case. The nurse brought her dinner, which she wouldn't touch, around four thirty. While she stared at the wall, I stared at her back. I wondered exactly what had happened and what effect this was going to have on her. You'd never guess it, but before this morning, Jillian was one of the most animated, independent, determined women I had ever met. She had had some rough times since we'd been together---her favorite aunt died; her car had been broken into and her purse was stolen; a big deal fell through; she had had a cyst removed from her ovaries and her gyno was talking hysterectomy---and she had been a little down. Nothing like this, thought, this despondency that I could see in her body language and in her eyes.

Dr. Sid Ferrera, MD

I got the x-rays back about two thirty and everything appeared to be normal. There weren't any other foreign objects in her body that I needed to worry her over. Physically, she was fine, but her mental health, I didn't feel, was quite right. I told her that I still wanted to keep her overnight, to be on the safe side. She stared at the wall. The boyfriend was still with her, which gave me hope that he hadn't done something and dumped her when things got out of control. She merely nodded her head in response to what I was telling her.

Raymond

I didn't think that the psychologist or psychotherapist or whatever was going to show. Time crawled by. I wanted to check in with Marge, my assistant, but couldn't find my cell phone. I checked all my pockets, but I don't know where it was. I had either left it in the car or dropped it at Jillian's. Don Delany had rescheduled the meeting for tomorrow morning. I already had a nine o'clock with a potential new client and three other phone meetings. Since she hadn't been able to get in touch with me, Marge had already reshuffled my entire week. Now if I could get Jillian out of here, everything would be back to normal. I stayed until about seven before I kissed her good night and headed home. I promised that I'd be back first thing in the morning.

Lily Perry, psychotherapist

I got to Jillian's room about eight p.m. Jillian was alone when I knocked. I pulled up a chair along side the bed and explained to her that Dr. Ferrera had asked me to stop by and chat.

'He doesn't believe me, does he?' she asked me when I had opened my notebook.

I asked her why she would think that.

'He doesn't believe there really was a phone call. He thinks Raymond had something to do with it.'

What makes you think that, I asked.

She sat up and crossed her legs Indian-style on the bed. 'Something in his attitude.'

Do you want to tell me what happened?

'Can I go home if I do?'

I told her that that decision wasn't up to me. And besides, if someone had made her hurt herself, why would she want to go back there tonight?

'It's my home,' she said.

We sat there for a few minutes, only the heating unit and the traffic in the hallway making any noise.

She ran her hands through her hair, tied it into a little knot at the base of her neck and took a deep sigh. She opened her mouth a couple of times, but nothing came out. I watched her as she fidgeted with the covers and played with the strands of hair that had come undone. She was highly agitated; Sid had made a wise decision in keeping her overnight. Jillian took another deep sigh, looked toward the window and began to speak.

Jillian

This morning, was it only this morning, about six forty, when the phone rang. I was still asleep since my first appointment wasn't until eleven; I had a closing for Gladstone at Western Title Company.

The first thought that ran through my head was that something had happened to my parents, then I figured Raymond might have forgotten something; he had an important meeting with the senior management at Delany & Associates that morning. It was on its fourth ring by the time I scooted across the bed and picked up the receiver.

A man identified himself as being affiliated with the phone company. They were having some problems on the line, were outside working, and I wouldn't be able to receive any incoming phone calls. He even identified me by name: Ms. Peabody.

I said okay and hung up. I remember that I thought that it wouldn't be a problem because my friends and family know better than to call me that early.

I had gotten back on my side of the bed when it rang again. Since I was more awake this time, I picked it up on the second ring.

It was the same voice: sharp, deep, masculine and without any trace of an accent. He said that they could see inside the house, that they were watching every move I was making and that as long as I did ething he told me too, they wouldn't come in, that I wouldn't get hurt.

'Do you understand me, Ms. Peabody?' he asked.

I said yes.

'Is there any money in the house, Ms. Peabody?'

I hesitated. This is when I knew I was being robbed. I remember thinking how clever this is.

'Quickly, Ms Peabody. Time is of the essence. Is there anyone in the house with you, a husband, a boyfriend, kids?'

I said no, that I was alone. I knew right after I said it that that was a big, big, big mistake.

'Is there any money in the house?'

'Ten dollars.'

'Are you sure that is all?'

'Yes, it's right here on my bed table. It might be eleven or twelve, but all I have is right here.'

'Are there any drugs in the house?'

I hesitated again.

'Quickly, Ms. Peabody. You do not want us to come in and take a look around, do you?'

'No!' I said. 'No, there aren't any drugs in the house. I mean there's aspirin and some cold tablets, and maybe some cough medicine, but no drugs. Not the good kind.'

'Here is what I want you to do.'

I didn't answer, holding my breath.

'Ms. Peabody?'

I barely breathed a 'yes.'

'Ms. Peabody, what is your first name?'

'Jillian.'

'Okay, Jillian, take a pillowcase off the bed.'

'Uh.'

'Now, Jillian. Do what I tell you and it will all be over in a few minutes. Take a pillowcase off the bed. Remember, I am watching.'

When I had it off, I said 'okay.'

'Put the money in the pillowcase.'

I fumbled on my night stand until I found the folded bill and threw it in the sack.

'Are you sure there is no more money in the house?'

'Yes.' The alarm clock went off. It was seven o'clock.

'Turn off the alarm. Do not look out the window. What about your purse?'

'It's in the living room; there may be some loose change in the bottom, but all the cash I have is right here.'

'Do you have any jewelry?'

'A little.'

'Get out of bed, but stay away from the windows. Do not look outside.'

I didn't answer.

'Do you understand me, Jillian? Do not look out the window.'

'Can I turn on a…'

'What did I say, Jillian? Do not look outside and it will all be over in a few minutes. Do you understand?'

'Yes.'

'Now put your jewelry in the pillowcase.'

I grabbed my amethyst ring and the diamond necklace Raymond gave me for Christmas that were lying on the bureau and threw them into the sack. Something in the back of my mind wouldn't let me put my diamond earrings in the sack or mention my jewelry case.

'Is that all?'

I nodded yes.

'Put your purse in the bag.'

'I have to put the phone down; it's in the living room.'

'Is there a phone in the living room?'

'Yes.'

'Is it a cordless?'

'Yes.'

'Put the phone on the bed, go pickup the other phone, then come back and hang up this phone. Take the pillowcase with you. If you take more than thirty seconds, we are coming in.'

I ran to living room, grabbed the phone, raced back to the bedroom and hung up the bedroom phone. 'Okay,' I said, panting.

'Go back into the living room and put your purse in the pillowcase. Stay away from the windows. Do not try to look outside.'

I ran back into the living room, but for some reason, I didn't get my purse. There was that nagging something again. I grabbed a little duffel bag I carry my heels in when the weather is bad and I wear sneakers to and from the office. 'Okay.'

'Is there any alcohol in the house, Jillian?'

'Uh, let me think. I don't drink, but...'

'Have you ever had two men have sex with you at one time, Jillian...one in the front and one in the back?'

'No!'

'You will if you do not quit fooling around. Now, is there any alcohol in the house?'

'Yes.'

'Where is it?'

'In the kitchen. In the cabinet above the refrigerator, but I can't remember what kind or how much'

'Jillian, go into the kitchen and take out the bottles.'

I ran into the kitchen and, standing on tiptoe, opened the cabinet.

'Tell me what is there and how much.'

I took out the first bottle. 'Rum. It's about half full.'

'Keep going.'

I took out other bottles---tequila, Crown Royal, and Schnapps---and said how much was in each. I lined them up carefully so that he could see them. As I was reaching in for the vodka bottle, the voice suddenly became more urgent.

'Hold the vodka up where I can see it.'

I held it out of the shadows and over the icebox.

'How much is in there?'

'It's about half full.'

'Jillian, I want you to open the bottle and take a nice long drink.'

I whimpered. I remember that. I whimpered. The voice became sharp again.

'Do it.'

I took a drink. It burned the back of my throat.

'Hold it up where I can see it.'

I held the bottle out in front of me. I could already feel the alcohol hitting my bloodstream, and my head, like a jackhammer.

'Take another drink. A nice, big drink this time. Nice and big.'

'I don't drink,' I whispered.

'Do it!'

There was that something again that told me that he couldn't really see inside. I put the bottle up to my lips, but I closed my teeth and let it run out the corners of my mouth.

'That's a good girl. Cap the bottle and put it in the bag.'

I did like he said; the pillowcase was much heavier now with the added weight of the vodka bottle and my sneaker bag.

'Are there any candles in the house?'

I nodded my head.

'Are there?'

'I was nodding, I'm sorry. Yes.'

'Where are they?'

'In the dining room.'

"Go into the dining room. Stay away from the windows. Do not try to look outside.'

Lily Perry, psychotherapist

Jillian stopped for a minute as if to pause. 'It's odd,' Jillian said. 'I think it's right about here that I remember thinking how he never used contractions.' She lay back down on the bed, then sat up again, her knees to her chest. 'I remember thinking how odd that was and that whoever was doing this was obviously well-educated.'

I made a few notes for Sid and maybe the police. After a few minutes, Jillian lay back down again. We sat there for a few minutes, only the heating unit and the traffic in the hallway making any noise. Then with a shake of her head, she started telling me her story again.

Jillian

I ran to the dining room, to the china hutch, pulled open the top right drawer, and rummaged inside. '"There's two." I said.'

'Put them in the bag and go back to the bedroom,' he said.

I stumbled back into the bedroom.

'Now Jillian, I want you to think. Are you sure there is not any more money in the house?'

'No, all I have is in the bottom of this bag.' I held the pillowcase up toward the window.

'Are you sure there are not any drugs in the house?'

'No, none. Some aspirin and cold medicine and stuff like that.'

'What about jewelry?'

'No, none.'

'Are you sure?'

'Wait! There's my jewelry box. I forgot about it. I'm sorry, I'm sorry. I was asleep when you called. Please don't hurt me; I forgot. Honest.' I ran across the room and flung open the two small doors.

'Put it all in the bag.'

I began to pull out strings of fake pearls, beads, all types of costume jewelry. I began to ask about the lapel pins, the glob of safety pins, the dried rose, but he cut me off.

'Put everything in the sack. We will decide what we want and leave the rest.'

There it was again, that nagging voice telling me not to open the top drawer where I kept my mother's diamond and ruby ring, my real pearl earrings and the real pearl necklace my parents gave me for my thirtieth birthday. So I didn't. I opened the bottom drawer and took out more costume jewelry, all that was in there and threw it into the pillowcase. '"I'm done,"' I said when I had finished.'

'Are you sure?'

I held my breath, terrified that he could see that I was lying. 'Yes.'

'Good. Now get a pair of panties out of your underwear drawer.'

This is when I heard the train, a passing locomotive. Brief, but unmistakable.

'What does the label say? If it does not match what you say when we get the pillowcase, we are going to come back. Understand?'

I must not have answered, because his voice rose a notch.

'Do you understand?'

'Yes.'

I reached for the pair on top and fumbled until I found the label. 'They're navy blue, cotton, the label is washed out; they're old. If you look hard enough, you'll see that the label is from Victoria's Secret. I buy all my underwear there.'

'Get out one of your bras and tell me what size and the label.'

I reached for the only clean bra that was in the drawer. 'The label's faded here too, but it's Victoria Secret. It's a 36D.'

'Put them in the bag. Remember, we will know if you are lying.'

I did like he said, then stood there. My head was swimming. I felt like I was going to pass out. I could hear my breath coming in hard gulps.

'It is almost over. Now take the candles out of the pillowcase and put them on the bed.'

I said okay when I had completed the task.

'Quickly, now. 'Put the pillowcase outside the front door. Keep your head down. If you try to see us, you will force us to hurt you.'

I ran to the front door, switching the pillowcase to my left hand and holding the phone to my ear with my right. I don't know how I managed so easily, but I flipped the deadbolt off, unhooked the chain and opened the door wide enough to get my hand and the bag through. I tried as hard as I could to keep my head behind the door. I let go of the pillowcase and shut the door as fast as I could. I heard it hit the porch as I was shutting the door.

'That is a good girl, Jillian. We will take what we want and leave the rest.'

"Okay," I said. "Can I hang up now?"

'No, Jillian, I have one more thing I need you to do. Run back to the bedroom.'

I think I said okay when I got back there, but I'm not sure. It doesn't matter if I did or not. He seemed to know where I was at all times.

'Now push all the covers off the bed, take off your pajamas, then lie down on your back.'

I knew at that precise moment, way down deep inside my core of me, that neither he nor anyone else could see inside my house. I don't wear pajamas or a nightgown. If he had been able to see in the house, he would have known that; I had been doing everything he told me to naked. It didn't register, like a part of me knew it, but the rest of me was still terrified.

'Take the jar of moisturizer off your night stand, get a big handful and put it on your stomach.'

Here again I knew down in my bones that he couldn't see in because he asked me which candle was the largest. If he could see in, then he would know, right? It was like I was under his control now and it didn't matter what I thought. Nothing registered except his instructions.

'Rub the candle in the cream, Jillian. Get it all nice and greased up.'

Lily Perry, psychotherapist

Jillian stopped talking again. I was anxious to ask her why she didn't hang up and call the police, but I wanted to make she sure was finished telling the story. That was important, that she tell it all to someone.

She fussed around on the bed, wouldn't make eye contact with me nor say anything else. We sat in silence for a full five minutes, with only the traffic in the hallway making any noise. The heating unit kicked on again.

Finally, she said, 'Well, I guess you can imagine what happened next.'

I answered that I only knew what Dr. Ferrera had told me.

'That's pretty much it.'

I didn't think she was going to say exactly what happened. Her face turned a bright red as if she were embarrassed by what she had gone through. I waited a few seconds and she continued.

'After he made me…after he made me…After it was over, he had one more thing to say before he let me hang up. '

Jillian broke down and began sobbing. I put my hands on her clasped ones and let her cry until she gave out.

Jillian

After I did what…after I did what he wanted me to, he said that I was to consider it a Monday morning prank and that I was not to call anybody, especially the police. Then he hung up. He made me do that to myself, then he hung up. It was a prank! I laid there for a few seconds, long enough for that voice recording from the phone company that says "If you want to make a call…."

I threw the phone down on the bed and ran back into the living room. My cell phone was plugged in next to the coffee table. I grabbed it and called Raymond to come over. I know it took about five minutes, maybe longer, for Marge, his assistant, to get him and at least another twenty minutes, maybe longer, for us to talk and for him to get here.

I don't even remember talking to him. One minute I was punching in his office number and the next he was running through the door. I have absolutely no idea what happened from the time Marge said, "Good morning, Delany and Associates. Raymond Henson's office," to the time Raymond walked through the door.

Lily Perry, psychotherapist

Jillian was blowing her nose when I asked her what she had thought when the voice told her to take the candles out of the bag.

"I only remember thinking that I didn't want two guys forcing themselves on me, that I've never had anal sex before and that I didn't want to get hurt."

Then I asked her why she didn't hang up. Her head snapped up and her eyes seemed to go dead.

"I have no idea," she said.

She seemed genuinely surprised that simply hanging up could have ended the whole thing. "It never occurred to me. I assumed that...that...that he could see everything that I was doing, even though a part of me knew better. Who would do a thing like that? And why me?"

Unfortunately, I had no answers to her questions. She lay back down on the bed and began sobbing again. I patted her shoulder, handed her some more Kleenex and waited. The traffic in the hallway had diminished significantly since it was past visiting hours and the heating unit kicked on again.

The night nurse came in around nine and gave her a sleeping pill. She stopped sniffling and finally fell asleep about ten. I tiptoed out about ten-fifteen.

Jillian

You know what the worst part is? I have a gun, a .38, and I didn't even think about it. It's lying in my bottom bureau drawer beneath my purple cashmere sweater. I didn't even have it loaded. The bullets are in a box next to it. Dad got it for me before he and Mom moved to Florida.

The fact that I probably could have stopped the whole thing by getting the gun out didn't even cross my mind. It didn't even cross my mind!

Raymond

After I left the hospital, I drove around for a while. I thought about going to the police, but what did I know at this point? Jillian had gotten a phone call from somebody who had threatened her and pretended to rob her and that it appeared that someone had made her do something to herself with a candle that had made her bleed. I didn't want to think about what she had done to herself with those candles.

I didn't know what to do. Finally, I stopped at this corner bar in Lafayette Square and had a beer. I was between a rock and a hard place, no cliché intended. If I postponed my meeting with Don Sr., I could kiss my career at Delany & Associates good-bye. Don was an old-timer; a seventy-year-old man who believed that work came first.

I've waited all my life for a woman like Jillian. Hell, I was almost forty-five. I'd been married once, when I was in my twenties, but that was a long time ago. I don't know. I had another beer before I drove home.

I couldn't sleep. I got up and tried to watch some TV, mostly for the company as actually trying to watch anything and mostly I surfed. I kept going over and over what had happened to Jillian and how this might change her. And us.

About midnight, I got out the phone book and called the phone company. Maybe they could trace the call or something. After what seemed like a long wait, How many people could be calling customer service this time of night? for a Customer Service Agent, I inquired about how I would go about tracing a phone call that was made to 314-657-8256.

The Agent told me that the information was confidential. Since my name wasn't on the account, for security reasons, she couldn't release any information.

I understood, even appreciated, that level of security. I inquired if Jillian could get the information. She said that she could tell Jillian if a phone call was made to that number but, due to privacy laws, the name and number of the caller was unattainable.

I was surprised. The privacy of a possible thief and God knows what else was protected, but Jillian's weren't? That made no sense to me. On the other hand, what I learned convinced me I had to go to the police, despite Jillian's reluctance.

I looked up the number to the Third Precinct and talked with the Officer who was on duty. I can't remember his name now. According to the log, he told me, a Dr. Sid Ferrera had already spoken to Detective Quinlan Moynihan.

That shocked me. Why would the doctor have called the police? Did he think I had done that to Jillian? Hell, I'm not even sure exactly what did happen to her, and I'm almost afraid to find out.

The Officer told me that Moynihan usually arrives between six-thirty and seven a.m. I left a voice mail message, saying that I would be dropping by.

Detective Quinlan Moynihan

I had only been in the office about ten minutes when Raymond Henson came in. His dark skin that had that leathery look of one too many suntans and coal-black crewcut with a sliver of gray running down the middle, almost like a skunk. He had deep crevices that ran from his nose to his chin, bushy eyebrows, and hadn't shaved.

He gave me the same basic story as Dr. Ferrera had yesterday. He wanted me to do something, but he wasn't sure what.

I told him that a crime report hadn't been filed and until then, there wasn't anything I could do for him.

We discussed whether a crime had actually been committed. He wasn't really sure and until I could talk more with the doctors, neither was I. He was concerned about the Southside Rapist, but I assured him that Dennis Rabbitt was safely behind bars without the possibility of parole. We talked about the crime scene as such and whether or not such a feat of seeing into someone's home was possible.

Unfortunately, I had to tell him, all sorts of spying equipment are available to the public. There's even a kiosk in Union Station, I forget the name of it, "S" I think it's called, where tiny cameras, voice recorders and whatnot can be bought rather inexpensively.

I agreed to meet him at Jillian Peabody's residence at 34856 Lanchester Avenue in St. Louis Hills later that morning for a quick look-see.

Raymond

I was a little surprised by Quinlan Moynihan's looks. With a name like that, I expected red hair, freckles, and a pale complexion. I also expected a heavy Irish brogue. Instead, he looked like a younger Robert Redford with St. Louis accent. I resisted the urge to ask him where he went to high school, which is a common St. Louis practice to quickly determine a person's socioeconomic background.

After I left Moynihan's office, I went to the office for my meeting with Don Sr. I dialed Jillian's room from my cell phone, but I couldn't hit the 'send' button. There was this huge knot in my stomach. I wasn't quite sure if I was up to either talking budgets with Don Sr. or facing what I thought had happened to Jillian.

I went straight to Don Sr.'s office, bypassing Marge and her quizzical nature. He didn't ask if everything was okay, but I didn't expect him too. During the meeting, I had trouble concentrating. Was Jillian thinking I had deserted her? Don Sr. noticed that I kept looking at my watch. The vein that runs across the top of his bald head was throbbing in sync with the movement of my watch's minute hand; it angered him that anything short of death could be more important than next year's budget and profit forecast.

Finally the meeting ended. I should have gone back to my office. I bet there was a pile of messages from clients and employees, but I didn't want to face Marge with her questions for which I had no answers. Again I dialed Jillian's room number, but I still couldn't make myself actually place the call. Maybe it would be better if I met Moynihan first, then I'd have something, anything to tell her.

Jillian

Jillian awoke around seven-thirty as the new shift nurse brought her breakfast. "Can I go home now?"

The nurse patted her shoulder. "The doctor will be in later this morning." She consulted the small erasable on the wall. "Dr. Ferrera makes his rounds close to lunchtime."

Jillian's shoulders sagged. She wanted to go home now. After moving the scrambled eggs and bacon around on the tray without eating a bite, she took her overnight bag and went to the bathroom to clean up. She was forced to take a sponge bath because there was no shower in the tiny bathroom. She thought about washing her hair in the sink, but she hadn't brought the hair dryer.

By eight-thirty, while Raymond was in his meeting, Jillian was sitting on the edge of the bed, watching the time tick slowly forward. By nine o'clock she was pacing the floor.

Lily Perry, psychotherapist

I talked with Dr. Ferrera about ten a.m. I gave him a brief detail of my session with Jillian. I disagreed with him that she and her partner, Raymond, had been involved in any type of sexual experimentation.

In my opinion, she was indeed suffering from Post Traumatic Stress Syndrome, but she needn't remain hospitalized. Without a complete psychiatric profile, I wouldn't be able to determine the long-term affects of her, her, I don't even know what to call it. It wasn't rape so to speak, nor was it guilt for taking pleasures in what is considered perverse sex.

I recommended that she be released with a prescription for some sedatives to help her sleep and the names of two or three psychiatrists and psychotherapists.

Detective Quinlan Moynihan

I met Mr. Henson at Jillian Peabody's house about eleven-thirty. I walked around the exterior, but there was no apparent sign of forced entry. I didn't see any evidence that someone had tried to place surveillance equipment in the bushes or on the gutters, but they can make those things so small now that it could take most of the Crime Scene Unit to find it.

We walked up to the front door. Again, no apparent sign of forced entry. As he got his keys out, I asked him to put on a pair of latex gloves before he touched the doorknob. He looked a little startled at my request, but seem to be okay with it once I started to also put on a pair.

Mr. Henson let us in and everything appeared to be in place. There weren't any broken windows. We went into the kitchen where he pointed out the open cabinet and the alcohol bottles all neatly lined up in a row. I checked the basement door and the door leading out to the deck, but they were secure and didn't appear as if anybody had tampered with them.

Then we walked down the hallway and peered into each of the two bedrooms. When we reached the last room at the end of the hallway, I could feel the tension rising in Mr. Henson.

We walked in and he pointed out the pillowcase and the blood on the bed. I squatted down to see inside the pillowcase. I pulled out what appeared to be some sort of book bag and a bottle of vodka.

Mr. Henson shrugged. "I don't know, I said. All I know is what I told you." The blood was dried---it was blood---and there seemed to be quite a bit. I asked him if he was sure that this was Ms. Peabody's blood and he nodded yes. Here in the bedroom, there were still no signs of forced entry or that a struggle had taken place. I checked the two windows; both were locked securely. Since there was nothing else to see, we left the house.

After locking up, we stood on the sidewalk and discussed options. I told him I could have a forensics team come over and take a sample of the dried blood to verify that it was indeed Ms. Peabody's and if it was menstrual blood or not.

He ran his hand over his head. I could see him trying to think back when Ms. Peabody's last cycle had occurred. He hadn't thought that it could be menstrual blood, but it was a definite possibility.

I told him that what happened next was really up to Ms. Peabody. If she wanted to file a report all she had to do was come down to the station. We shook hands and parted.

Raymond

I got to the hospital about one-thirty. Jillian was pacing the floor, anxious to get out of there. She had called her employer and let him know that she was sick, had been throwing up all morning and that she would spend the rest of the day in bed.

'I don't want him to know,' she told me. 'I don't want anybody to know about this.'

What about calling the police and making a report?

'No way,' she said. 'I said that I don't want anyone knowing about this. Especially my family. Or yours.'

I didn't think this would be a good time to tell her I had already been to the police. I let her pace. When will the doctor be in? I asked, anxious to move the subject from the police.

'The nurse said he did his rounds around lunch.' She stopped and looked at the clock. 'He should have been here by now.'

Maybe he had an emergency or something, I said.

Jillian shot me her *Raymond, you can be so stupid sometimes* look. I watched her pace a while, then flipped on the TV and surfed.

She paced about three lengths of the room before she said anything. Then it was

"Why don't you go on back to your place."

I was completely taken aback. First I kinda stared at her, then I asked her if she didn't want me to take her home.

"No," she said. "I'll call a taxi. I want to be alone."

I tried to argue, gently of course, with her, saying that it might be dark by the time she was released, that she might be afraid once she got to the house, that once she got there, she might not want to be in the house alone. What if there really was some lunatic watching her house?

"No," she said. "I don't think there is. And if there is, what can you do about it?"

Well, I answered, I could call the police, there's greater safety in numbers, especially when the other person is a man or I could simply be there. I tried to persuade her to at least call her best friend, Anita, to take her home or to meet her there and spend the night with her.

She was adamant about going it alone, her hardheadedness suddenly rearing its bronze head. I grabbed my overcoat and left. I would have slammed the door if I could have!

Dr. Sid Ferrera, MD

It was approximately four o'clock when I reached Room 447. A school bus accident on Forest Park Boulevard involving several kindergartners kept me in ER much of the day.

Jillian seemed nervous and agitated when I arrived, which was vastly improved over yesterday's apathy. When I was all the way in the room, she put her hands on her hips and demanded to know when she could leave.

I asked her to sit down and noticed that she did so gently. Does your rectum still hurt?

She nodded and shrugged, "It's a little sore."

I asked her if she had had a bowel movement since the incident yesterday.

She shook her head no. "Can I go home now?"

I saw no reason to keep her. I wrote her two prescriptions, one for a laxative, the other for sleeping pills. Then I signed the release papers and told her the nurse would be there shortly to escort her out. I told her that she could call Mr. Henson; she would be ready in about a half-hour. She said nothing, so I left.

Jillian

Darkness came early in January. By the time the taxi arrived at the hospital's South Entrance, the streetlights had come on. It was a short twenty-minute ride from the Barnes Jewish Hospital to Jillian's house in St. Louis Hills. She noted the neat, winter-ready lawns, the expensive cars in the drives. The taxi pulled up in front of her three-bedroom ranch at 34856 Lanchester Avenue.

Jillian jerked awake to the phone ringing. Pushing her hair out of her face, she sat up and watched it ring. Twice. Three times. Four times. She knew she should pick it up. There was no use in trying to hide. Let it go, she thought. It's done, it's over and there's nothing you can do about it.

On the sixth ring, Jillian took a deep breath and answered the phone. She'd show them, she thought. "Hello," she said, desperately trying to sound as if she hadn't a care in the world. Then she waited, her lungs beginning to ache.

"Did I interrupt anything?"

Jillian sagged with relief. It was her mother. Gladys Peabody never started one of their phone conversations with 'Hello.' She assumed that her daughter would recognize her voice.

"No, Mother," Jillian said. "I feel asleep watching the news. I'm glad you called. What are you up to tonight?"

The women covered the weather and the imminent ice storm, which were Gladys' major concern, and Raymond. Jillian asked about her father.

As was his style, Fred Peabody got on the phone and said a few words to his only daughter before handing the phone back to Gladys.

Gladys asked about Jillian's job.

Before Jillian could reply, it sounded as if someone picked up another phone to join the conversation. Jillian reached for the gun and held it in her hand. She looked over her shoulder and around the room.

"Fred, hang up the phone," Gladys shouted.

"I did," Jillian heard him shout back.

He's back, Jillian thought as her parents argued half a country away. He's back. He's going to know I called Raymond and he's going to come in.

The phone connection began to break up and the sound of someone picking up and hanging up another phone was continual. "Sounds like some of the lines are being crossed," Jillian told her mother. "This is giving me a headache; I'll call you tomorrow."

While Jillian removed the gun from its leather holster, the women said their *I love you's* and *goodnight's* over the clicks of the phone wires.

Jillian grabbed the gun and ran to her bedroom. With her back against the outer wall, she slid down until the gun rested on her knees. Let 'em come in, she thought to herself, let anybody walk through that door.

Julie Failla Earhart

Death in the Afternoon

"Yes, Officer, I was the one who found the body."

"No, Officer, I didn't kill---what was it, a man or a woman?"

"No sir, I didn't kill her."

"My name is George Richard Kincaid, Jr. Everybody who knows me calls me Jack."

"I don't know why."

"I was looking for my mitten when I saw it."

"Why, I'm 45, Officer. Does that matter?"

"Lots of people wear mittens. They're warmer ya know."

"No, first I saw that big red stain in the snow I told you about."

"I don't know. I figured some kid had spilled his Kool-Aid or something."

"Yeah, well, that's what I thought at first."

"Then I saw it---I mean her. You did say it was a her, didn't you, Officer?"

"Well, I can't remember if I started yelling for help first or ran up to her first and then started yelling. Uh, can I bring that trashcan over here, Officer, I, uh, I think I'm, uh, going to throw up."

"Yes, I'd appreciate a glass of water."

"Okay. I'm ready now. Can I start over? I need to start over."

"When I saw it---I mean her. I was walking down the sidewalk—at least I think it was the sidewalk. With all that snow it was hard to say---looking for my mitten. Then I saw a big red stain on the snow. Then I saw it---I mean her. Then I ran over to her and then I started yelling for help. Yeah, I remember now. I ran up to her, and when I saw what had happened, I started yelling. "

"What happened? I don't know how it---I mean her---I mean I don't know how she got there, Officer, I know what I saw."

"It was so gross, there was blood everywhere. Her head was lying about two feet from the rest of her body."

"It was awful, Officer, I bet I have nightmares about this forever."

"No, she wasn't wearing any clothes. Had a nice figure though, firm breas---"

"I did not touch them! I wouldn't do that! They looked like they would be, that's all!"

"I forgot it was a woman! I forget a lot of things! I forgot. That's all! You made me remember."

"You're confusing me!"

" No, I never saw her before."

"There weren't any panties in my coat pocket."

"Well, they don't belong to me."

"I don't wear girl's clothes."

"I did not ask her for sex!"

"The last time I had sex? I can't remember."

"I think it was right before I went into the hospital last time. I'm not sure."

"I CAN'T REMEMBER!"

"I'm sorry, I didn't mean to yell. You're making me nervous. Can I have another cup of water?"

"Thanks. Okay, I'm better now. I forgot it was a woman until you had me remembering, that's all, Officer. Honest, I forgot."

"Please don't make me remember anymore."

"I was so scared. All that blood and stuff. Of course as soon as I saw it. I knew it wasn't Kool-Aid; it was blood. It's only logical, and there was so much of it. So much. I didn't know people had that much blood in 'em."

"What? I'm sorry Officer, but I feel really weird right now. Like I'm floating on a cloud or something. Or maybe lying on one. I kinda like it. It feels good—in a strange sort of way. I'm not perverted in any way;

I'm not. Don't get the wrong idea about me. I feel really odd right now. Maybe I took too much of my medication again. Sometimes I can't remember if I've taken it or not, so I take it again. Usually I have, and then I feel weird like this. So I must have."

"Haldol. Fifty milligrams twice a day."

"About eight months."

"Lots of different things. Lithium. Thorazine. Prozac. Haldol seems to work the best. Everyone says they've noticed the difference. Or maybe I ate too much Mexican food last night. My mouth loves spicy foods, but my stomach, well, my stomach hates Mexican food and usually rebels. I was surprised I didn't throw up; I usually do when I eat Mexican food, but it's so good going down. Or did I have those nachos for lunch? That's funny, I can't remember when I ate last. I try to never miss a meal. Plays havoc with my medicine, ya know?"

"I'm sorry, Officer, would you repeat that?"

"Start at the beginning. Oh, okay."

"I don't remember much until I was on my way to work, and I was feeling strange. Kinda like I do right now. It was weird. I didn't think I was really outside; I thought I was having a dream or something. There was nothing but whiteness. Like that time I was caught in that blizzard in Michigan. It was scary."

"Yeah, I know now that I was outside. The other officer told me. This is the second blizzard I've been caught in. Bet that doesn't happen to many people, huh?"

"Upper Peninsula."

"1983. Or maybe it was '84. I can't remember, although you'd think that a person would remember when they were trapped in a blizzard, huh? I got a feeling that blizzards are gonna be the death of me yet."

"Oh, I'm sorry, Officer. Well, I was taking a shortcut through Central Park, hurrying a little slower than usual toward my job at the art museum, trying to watch the teeny-tiny snowflakes drift through the tree limbs. I could've enjoyed it better if I hadn't overslept that morning, but let's face it. I'm not a morning person. On good days it takes me a good half hour to drag my bones from beneath the covers, and on bad days, when I'm not feeling good, well, I don't make it up at all. Sometimes I can't even call the museum, but they understand. It was part of the deal."

"The hospital worked it out with them. I do my job as best I can, but I can't always make it in. They're nice people; they understand."

"The longest? Let me think. The longest I can ever remember staying in bed is six days. The Haldol helps; it really does. I haven't missed a day since I started taking it. Well, except for today, and I got lost, what with the snow and all."

"Sorry, I have a tendency to ramble. There I was in the park, the snow starting to fall, and, ya know the weirdest part, I didn't see another living soul. No one was in the park but me and the snow. It was strange 'cause you and I both know that New Yorkers never let a little bit of snow stop 'em. So that was really spooky. Not even the squirrels were hanging around for leftovers. I started walking a little faster 'cause I was scared of being alone like that and 'cause if you're in the park too long, you stand a good chance of getting mugged."

"Me? I've only been mugged six times in the four years I've lived here. Not bad considering I cross the park at least twice a day. I bet that--"

"The last time? About six months ago, I think. Yeah, six months. I remember 'cause I was wearing--"

"No, it really doesn't make me mad. Nobody has ever hurt me though. If they hurt me, I might get mad."

"No, I wasn't mad at that woman. She didn't do anything to hurt me. If she had hurt me, I'd remember her."

"I never saw her before I saw her lying there in the snow."

"Well I can't help it if other people have seen her walking in the park every morning. I never have. I try to mind my own business."

"No, she didn't try to mug me."

"No, she didn't ask me if I wanted to have sex with her."

"I told you I never saw her before."

"Oh okay. Well, the snow started falling faster and faster and the flakes were getting bigger and bigger. The wind had picked up too, whipping little pieces of ice that were mixed in with the snow right into my face. Wouldn't ya know that was the one day that I forgot my scarf?"

"That looks like my scarf, but it's not."

"I forgot it."

"It was lying on the ground beside her?"

"I have a confession to make, Officer. I didn't really forget my scarf. Jupiter, that's the cat who lives upstairs in old lady Benson's apartment, was sleeping on it, and that overweight hairball hates me so much that he spits at me whenever I get too close, so I let him finish his nap."

"No it's not mine. Can I have it if nobody else claims it? That way I wouldn't have to worry about ol' Jupiter getting car hair all over it. I'm allergic to cat hair. Funny thing though, Jupiter is old lady Benson's cat, but she doesn't claim it. She says Jupiter belongs to the universe. Me, I say Jupiter belongs to her if she feeds it—I don't know if that ol' cat is a boy or a girl, so I call it an 'it.' Personally, I think that she told Jupiter to hate me like she does. She always looks at me funny because of the voices."

"Well, sometimes I hear voices, and if I forget where I am, which happens a lot, I talk back. I know it makes people uncomfortable, but it's that I forget that other people don't hear 'em."

"It's been a while. I really think it's the Haldol, Officer. It sure seems to help."

"The museum? I work in the basement so I usually don't see anybody. That was part of the deal, too."

"They didn't want me bothering people. In case I forgot where I am."

"No, I don't mind. It's kinda lonely though. And dark. I hate it when Ken---"

"The night security guard. When he turns out the light, and it's dark when I get down there."

"Yeah, I know it's sissy, but I'm scared of the dark."

"Bad things happen in the dark."

"Bad things."

"Okay. Well, that big ol' cat was curled up on my scarf, and I didn't know it was supposed to snow or I would've maybe tried to get it. Anyway, by the time I reached the entrance to the zoo, I could barely see my hand in front of my face. My heart was beating so hard I swear I could see my coat moving. My palms were sweating through my mittens. I stopped to catch my breath and check my pulse. A little faster than normal, but the hardness of the pounding started to worry me. I could be having a heart attack!"

"No, I've never had a heart attack, Officer, but I read about it happening to a guy in Montana. His heart started beating real hard, then real hard and fast-- like mine was doing--while he was in the woods. And he died!"

"No, I'm not afraid of dying; in fact, I'm ready for it. I tried to go a couple of times, but I guess heaven wasn't ready for me. I don't think I'll try it again though. There are still a lot of things I want to do."

"Well, I would like to have a girlfriend, and go to college, and write a play, and go to Ohio and Paris, and discover a Da Vinci beneath some of that God-awful stuff in the pop art collection and learn Hungarian. Mom—God rest her soul—said that my dad came from Hungary in the mid-fifties but was deported about two weeks before I was born."

"My dad was a Communist?!"

"Oh, I'm sorry. I thought you meant that he was."

"I never did think to ask her why until after she was dead, then it was too late."

"We tried to find him off and on while I was growing up but we never got a reply. Mom always supposed he was dead."

"The hospital said they sent a message to the Red Cross when Mom died, but if they found him, I never heard from him."

"Nah, I don't think I'll try to find him."

"If he didn't want me before he even knew me, I'll bet you a hundred dollars he won't want me now."

"Well, I'm not exactly, ah, normal, ya know."

"Okay. So, there I was, alone, in the middle of Central Park, my heart galloping like a race horse, barely able to see, the snow whirling and swirling around me, the wind howling around my ears, thinking I was having a heart attack. I couldn't remember what to do. Should I run toward the street, or should I lie down right there and wait for it to pass? I was pretty sure that lying down would be certain death---I can't die yet; I told you how much I have left to do---so I took off in the direction of Fifth Avenue, but somewhere I managed to take a wrong turn, and I kept heading deeper and deeper into the park. The snow was coming down faster and faster and starting to pile up on the sidewalk, the benches, and what was left of the grass. It kept sticking to my eyelashes and melting in my eyes so I lowered my head. That was a mistake 'cause then I didn't see the missing section of concrete until I tripped, tearing my jeans and scrapping my knee. That's how I must have lost my left mitten."

"You found it? Great! Can I have it back? Look at how chapped my hand is. I have sensitive skin, Officer, and being out in that storm chapped my poor little hand."

"Well, I don't know how the dead lady got a hold of it. Maybe she found it and picked it up and was gonna keep it for herself."

"Maybe she was trying to put it on the wrong hand when whoever killed her did it to her. She could have been real stupid, Officer. You don't know if she was smart or stupid, do you, Officer?"

"Oh no, I wasn't implying anything."

"The other marks? What other marks? I didn't see any other marks, Officer."

"I don't know what stab wounds looks like."

"Like giant cigarette burns? That's odd, don't you think, Officer? How many were there?"

"SIXTY-FIVE!"

"That's something I'd like to ask you about Officer; I've always about that. Why would anyone stab somebody that many times when only once or twice would do?"

"Well, yeah, there was that incident at the hospital the last time I was there."

"He made me mad. I'm telling ya, Officer, that I don't hurt nobody unless they make me mad."

"He peed all over my paints and easels."

"I stabbed him."

"It was only a butter knife, Officer. He didn't even bleed."

"No, that's not all. First he told Dr. Traflagar that I wasn't doing as well as it looked, that I was only acting."

"Dr. Traflagar didn't believe him."

"Jealous I guess."

"'Cause I was getting out early. I was supposed to stay until the end of the month, but they were going to let me out a week early."

"Dr. Traflagar said I was doing better than he expected."

"That's what he told me. That and something about the insurance money running out."

"No, I don't own any pruning shears, but old lady Benson has a pair in the basement of the apartment building."

"That's them. How did you get them?"

"They have blood on them? I don't think I've used 'em since July when I cut down that rosebush for her."

"Everybody who lives in the building can borrow them anytime they want."

"Oh, okay. Where was I?"

"That's right. I had fallen over that missing section of concrete, and my knee was really hurting. I could feel a small trickle of blood inching its way down my leg. But I got up and kept on running—but it was more like limp-running. My knee was throbbing almost as hard as my heart was pounding. I still hadn't seen another person or even reached one of the Avenues, and I should have. No matter what, if you stay headed in one direction, you always come out of the park. It seemed like I was going in deeper and deeper and my heart was feeling like somebody had reached down my throat, grabbed it and was squeezing it like all get out. I was pretty sure I was going into cardiac arrest. Then I started getting dizzy and nauseous."

"But you said you wanted the whole story."

"Well, I thought the dizziness and nauseous was from lack of oxygen, running like I was. Then I remembered that Uncle Larry—my mom's little brother, that's what she always called him, her little brother, even though he was in his sixties the last time I saw him."

"Let me think. It's been about two years I guess. Anyway, Uncle Larry told me when I was visiting him in intensive care that was how he felt when he was having--"

"Dizzy and nauseous. When he was having his heart attack. He's the only family member I have left, so I didn't mind the train ride to Florida to see him. He told me all about it, in minute detail, 'cause I wanted to know since heart problems run on Mom's side of the family. The doctor said there was only minor damage, but still he decided to retire early. He was some sort of CFO for a paint company down there. Mom always said he was lazy so his retiring didn't surprise me. I think it surprised Aunt Vivian---"

"Oh, okay. Well, I had it on pretty good authority what a heart attack felt like--"

"No, I don't remember any weird stuff like that happening to my heart in Michigan. I think I had a blackout; I'm not real sure though."

"No, I don't have seizures."

"No, no family history of seizures that I know of. I could check my mom's medical records. I still have them. I keep them in a---"

"Blackouts? A couple."

"While I was in the hospital. It was while they were trying to get my medicine balanced."

"Okay. The snow was getting deeper, must have been an inch or so piled there on the top of the trash can. I got really scared when I saw that. I knew I wasn't in the park anymore, but I didn't know where I was."

"How did I know? You never see a trash can in Central Park that has a lid. I stopped to look around, but all I could see was snow. Soft billowy snow. Sort of like I was in the middle of a gigantic marshmallow. I even felt sticky, but I think that was 'cause I was sweating so hard from the running. My armpits were wet, my mitten was completely soaked---but I think a lot of that had to do with my falling earlier like I told you—and I could feel these two drops of sweat turtle racing down my spine."

"Turtle racing? That's two drops of sweat going real slow, Officer. You know on those really--"

"Okay. Where was I?"

"Yeah. The trash can lids. I started to get really scared 'cause I didn't know where I was. The snow was coming down so thick and hard that there weren't any spaces between the flakes. Sort like a giant cotton bedsheet—like the ones they use at the hospital---was falling from the sky."

"I come and go. When the voices get really loud, I have to go back to the hospital until they shut up for a while. Let's see, I think it's been almost a year since I was there. Ya know, I really miss ol'—"

"Sorry. I told you I had a tendency to ramble, so I don't mind when you yell at me like that. My mom used to do it all the time. Don't make me nervous; I can't remember when I get nervous."

"No, I don't get mad; I can't remember."

"So, I decided to sit down for a while. I brushed the snow off the bench with my mittened hand and it was kinda hard since I'm left handed, but I didn't want to take my hand out of my nice warm jacket pocket. I chap real easy. So I sat there and tried to figure out where I was. I was getting comfortable when I saw that man."

"I thought I told you about him before. Are you sure that I didn't?"

"I'm sorry, I should have. Please don't yell at me. I can't remember if you yell at me. I'm so stupid sometimes. My mom always said it was 'cause I talk too much and I do ramble a--"

"He was wearing a blue coat and a stocking cap. He was walking real fast toward me. Boy, was I glad to see him. I yelled at him but it was like he didn't hear me. I figured that because of the wind and snow that he couldn't hear me. So I stood up to wait for him so I could ask him where I was. People are usually pretty nice about telling me where I am. They look at me like they're scared of me though, and that's okay 'cause I'm used to it."

"Sorry. Please don't yell at me. While I was waiting, I checked my pulse again. It seemed like it almost back to normal. At least the pounding had stopped. And I didn't feel dizzy or nauseous anymore. It was so weird, when I looked up he was gone."

"I DO NOT SEE THINGS!"

"I DON"T KNOW! HE VANISHED INTO THIN AIR."

"I AM NOT GETTING UPSET!"

"Can I have some more water?"

"Thanks. Hey! Ya know something I thought of? Maybe he killed her? He was headed in that direction."

"It was weird. I thought maybe that I'd entered a twilight zone or something. Do you ever watch that show?"

"It gives me the creeps."

"The man? What man?"

"Oh, him. Well, I thought maybe he was an angel, although not a friendly one—or helpful for that matter."

"You don't believe in angels? Oh, pish-posh, Officer. How do you think we make it through the day without angels?"

"That's a great word, pish-posh, don't you think, Officer? Not one you hear much."

"Well, they're out there no matter what you think. I need to have a word with God about that."

"No, He never talks back."

"I don't know who the voices are, they've never said."

"I never thought to ask."

"Yeah, well. There I was, pretty certain that I wasn't going to die this time, and I was glad 'cause I have a lot--"

"Okay. So I started looking around, trying to figure out where I was. All there was whiteness, like I told you about before, and I was starting to get cold."

"Yeah, that's odd, isn't it, Officer, that I hadn't noticed the cold before. I had dressed really warm when I left my apartment. Maybe it was cause I had been sweating and with that cold wind whipping on it--"

"I'm trying to tell you what happened, Officer. You said you wanted the whole story and for me to start at the beginning."

"Well, I can't help it if I need to explain some things to you so that you'll understand."

"No I don't mean to imply that you're stupid, Officer. You don't know me that's all, and I want you to understand."

"I always tell the truth, Officer. Every time. I always get caught if I don't. Or I feel guilty. I always get caught when I lie. Like that time at the hospital when—"

"Fine. Where was I?"

"I was cold, and I was afraid my ears were getting frostbit, and I was lost, and I didn't know what to do. So I started walking back the way I came. I wanted to cry, but my mom taught me never to cry in public. I think that's a pretty---"

"No, she never let me play sports."

"She was always afraid that I'd get hurt."

"I wanted to. I wanted to be like the other guys, but Mom always said I was different."

"Yeah, I like girls."

"Not a steady girlfriend. Not like all the other guys had."

"All the girls laughed at me. They said I was weird and revolting. Besides, Mom wouldn't let me date."

"She said girls would take advantage of me and make me do things with them that was disgusting."

"I don't know."

"I didn't have sex until after Mom died."

"She would have been mad at me if I had."

"Of course not! She would never make me do that with her! She said it was disgusting!"

"MY MOM NEVER HAD SEX. SHE SAID IT WAS DISGUSTING!"

"Mom said the stork brings 'em."

"Yeah, I liked it. It felt good."

"Since then? Not often."

"Women laugh at me."

"I don't know."

"I don't know."

"I DON"T KNOW."

"The first time? With a nurse at the hospital."

"Yeah, she laughed, but she said she didn't care."

"I felt bad afterwards, though. Mom would have been mad at me."

"I don't remember the last time. I think it was right before I went into the hospital the last time, but I'm not sure."

"I told you I never saw that woman in the park before."

"Yeah, I guess she might have been pretty. I didn't notice what with her head being chopped off like that."

"I might have wanted to."

"I was at work yesterday."

"I swear, Officer, I was there. Call the museum; they'll tell ya."

"It's Friday, the 18th."

"Monday, the 21st? It can't be Monday. I do my laundry on Sundays and I don't remember doing it yesterday."

"I remember leaving my apartment for the museum and heading into the park."

"Okay. The night before. I left the museum and since there were a lot of other people around, I sort of took my time in the park. Strolling, I guess you'd call it."

"I didn't have any place in particular to be."

"Well, I sat down on the park bench and this real pretty woman walked by, so I said "hi," and she said, "hi," back. She had pretty red hair. Like that woman I found in the park."

"We talked."

"Stuff. Ya know. The trees, what I do at the museum, how I like to spend my time."

"She said she had seen me there before."

"Yeah, I told ya, remember, I spend a lot of time in the park."

"Then she asked me if I wanted to go back to her place."

"I said no."

"She might want me to do something disgusting with her."

"I don't know."

"She shrugged and we kept on talking."

"My stamp collection, and I told her all about how ol' Jupiter hates me, and she said she didn't like cats either and that she had a dog named Harold. I really like dogs. They're so much more fun than cats. Then she asked me if I wanted to help her take Harold for a walk and I---

Fountain of Youth

Jeb Larson grasped the bus' handrails and lowered himself slowly. His left foot waved in mid-air until it connected with the grooved steel step. When both feet were firmly planted, he let out a long-held breath.

"Hurry up, Pop," the driver said, reaching for the black padded grip which operated the doors. "I'm behind schedule."

"Gonna rain something fierce tonight," Jeb replied. "Hope you brung yo' umbrella."

The driver leaned forward and peered through the sun-soaked windshield. "There ain't a cloud in the sky, old man. Now get a move on."

"These ol' knees never lie." Jeb pointed to swollen joints beneath his dark brown trousers that, even on good days, were almost as round as the driver's head.

"Yeah, well, until then, I'm behind. Get a move on."

Jeb turned sideways and dangled a foot from the bus. He grunted as he eased it onto the sidewalk. "Now hold yo' britches and give me a minute 'afo you go tearin' outta here." As he placed the other foot tentatively on the sidewalk and began to move away, the driver slid-slammed the doors into place, and the bus lurched from the curb.

Jeb's walk was a mixture of shifting his body from side to side and shuffling his feet, thanks to the arthritis that had bowed his legs until they had formed an imperfect heart. Walking was slow and painful, but he absolutely refused to use a cane. Over the years, he'd given in to the hearing aid, the false teeth, the trifocals and the little purple pills that kept his blood pressure down, but he drew the line at using a cane. "Damn it all to hell," he'd swear whenever anyone had ever mentioned that it might be easier if he had a little help, "If I can't gets around on these two legs the good Lord done give me, then I don' need to be a goin' nowheres."

Other than the arthritis, which had first seized his body in early 1941, Jeb considered himself healthy for a ninety-five-year-old man. His son, Lawrence, however, disagreed. It had taken a lot of talking on Jeb's part to convince Lawrence that he didn't need to leave the retirement center for a nursing home after his heart attack three years ago.

"I gots to rest me a minute," Jeb said and leaned thick forearms against the rust and yellow dispenser of the *Atlanta Times-Democrat*. He ran a hand over white nape that was still plentiful on his head, then wiped the sweat on his baggy pants. His head hung over his arms, the bus's fumes and heat shimmering around him.

After he caught his breath, Jeb looked up at the street signs. Peachtree ran north and south; 171st spread east and west. He took the folded newspaper picture from his jacket pocket and flattened it gently. He studied the caption, white eyebrows drawing together over deep-set eyes and a wide nose, then looked up again at the street signs, matching the letters and the numbers with the ones in the picture. "This be the place all righty," he said.

Jeb pushed himself up and away and moved toward the concrete bench next to the bus stop sign. "I gots to rest me a minute more," he muttered as he eased himself onto the hard slab and pulled at the pale yellow windbreaker. He always wore the jacket, no matter the weather. "I's gots thin blood," he'd say to anyone who asked him why, even on the hottest of days, he wore the jacket. "I's gets cold easy and I's rather wear it than carry it."

He surveyed the four corners. Close to forty years had passed since he was in this part of Atlanta; the fountain had still been working then. "Don' recognize nothin' no more. Then, didn' rightly 'xpect t'."

Graffiti, ten feet high, covered red brick buildings, weathered plywood nailed shut windows, and iron bars guarded darkened doorways in what was once the South's largest garment district. Jeb watched as a car rolled past him, unidentifiable music booming through its open windows. Directly across the street, one of the iron-barred doors swung open. A young black man squatted in the doorjamb and lit a cigarette. By his bearing and agility, along with a black Oakland Raiders baseball cap, the bill sticking out to the left and pulled low over his forehead, Jeb thought he must be in his late teens or early twenties, but he couldn't tell.

Jeb lifted his face to the morning sun, the wrinkles on his ebony face falling into soft puddles around his ears. Beads of sweat rolled into the pleats of skin as Jeb let the memories have their way, the newspaper clipping held gently in his lap by a massive hand.

He could see himself at five, with Roland, one of his six brothers, splashing in the fountain's clear waters after a day of playing Civil War among the blackened ruins of the slave quarters where his great-grandparents had lived, three miles from the new house the Winchester's had built during Reconstruction. Jeb always played his, his daddy's, and his granddaddy's namesake, J.E.B. Stuart; Roland, older by three years, always played Sherman.

Once, the two little boys had been so focused on their game that they had accidentally set the woods on fire. Jeb chuckled as his mama's voice echoed in his ears as she yelled at them, her shaking finger pointed directly at Jeb's left nostril. Mama wasn't much of a disciplinarian, but Daddy, well, the boys knew what they were in store for when Daddy came in from the fields---and it sure wasn't a wagging finger.

The image shifted to his fifteen-year-old self spending his afternoons hoeing the long, lush rows of cotton, then scooping the fountain's cool water into a bucket and dumping it over his feet to clean the red clay which had stuck like socks.

Memories of his mother on her knees scrubbing Mr. Jeffrey's blood from the red bricks that made a circular pattern around the fountain, of the hounds lapping noisily from the pool after a night of cooning, of Roland fishing their two-year-old sister, Delilah, floating face down, from the transparent water, toppled over each other in their quest for center stage.

The ache in Jeb's neck forced him to lift his head, stopping the recollections that had been forcing themselves on him since Nurse Gimbel had shown him the fountain's picture in the *Times-Democrat*. He had recognized it right off when she asked him if he had ever heard of the Winchester plantation. The picture also triggered a memory. A memory that had been buried for around eighty-eight years. A memory of watching Granddaddy burying the family treasure.

Jeb had watched his grandfather and his father dig the hole for the fountain, the hot Georgia sun creating glistening streams on deep black backs that were almost as dark as his. He squatted beside the two men as they lay the circular pattern of red cobblestones that spread twenty feet from the fountain. It had taken the men almost eight weeks to dig through the hard clay and another six to lay the bricks. And all that time, Miss Molly, the plantation's last mistress, was hovering and fluttering around like a butterfly.

He stared hard at the clipping in his hand, then lifted his glasses and held the picture closer to his face. Miss Molly would be heartbroken if she could see what had become of her beloved fountain.

The fins on the three dolphins he could make out in the grainy photo had been broken off and the outstretched arm of a boy holding a jar had been sheared at the shoulder. He could see none of the intricate carvings that he knew covered most of the statue, the bronze had turned a moldy green, the pool was heaped with trash and leaves, and the edging cobblestones were cracked or had disintegrated into piles of red dust.

His eyes shifted to the caption. He had Nurse Gimbel read it over and over until he had memorized the words.

"The last remains of the Civil War-era Winchester plantation sits among ruined and abandoned buildings near Peachtree and 171st. The fountain and nearby buildings are scheduled for demolition next week to make way for a ten-unit strip mall, part of the campaign promise Mayor Clark made to help revitalize Atlanta's South Side."

Jeb shook his head and brought the picture closer to his face, his eyes almost crossing as he tried to stare at the cobblestones directly behind the stone boy. The image in Jeb's hand swam away.

"Granddaddy, why'd you dig up those two bricks you laid and diggin' a hole?" seven-year-old Jeb asked as he knelt beside the old man.

"Now youngun," Granddaddy said, wrapping rawhide strips around a wallet-sized leather pouch, "This heres our family treasure. I don' wants you to fo'get it's here ifn anything happens to me."

"What could happen, Granddaddy?" the child asked, wide eyes staring into the hole.

Granddaddy placed the pouch in the red clay and began to replace the bricks.

"What's in there?"

"Klan's been ridin' agin."

"Is it valu'ble like Miss Molly's ring?"

The boy watched as Granddaddy finished the job in silence.

"Now you run on," Granddaddy said, grunting as he pulled himself to his feet. "I gots chores t' finish an' it's almos' suppa time."

Jeb lowered the photo, shifted his glasses back into place, and looked around, not exactly sure where to start. The young black man he had seen earlier had disappeared and now the streets were empty. He wished he hadn't made the trip on a Saturday. Fifty years ago, even on Saturdays, a frenzied atmosphere had hung over the area, but today, the quiet was spooky. He shook his torso. "I gots to make me a plan," he muttered, "or I ain't ever gonna find it."

Folding the clipping carefully, Jeb placed it delicately in his pocket. He closed his eyes and tried to remember the layout of the area. He had spent twenty years living and working among the dilapidated shells that surrounded him, first as a runner for Talmadge Brothers Dress Company, then as an elevator operator after the arthritis bent his legs. He could see the fountain, as it was then, behind Curran's Hat Company, the water flowing gracefully, the pool deep and clear. And cold. Always cold.

Any o' these ol' buildin's could be Curran's, Jeb thought. That ol' fountain could be 'most anywhere around here.

He struggled to stand and looked around, hoping for some indication of where Curran's used to be. Holding on to the back of the bench with one hand, he shaded his eyes with the other and surveyed the area across the street. There were two buildings, an alley and another building. Jeb looked for the word "hat" in the faded signs. It was a word he knew; a word he could pick out in any newspaper, book, or magazine. None of the signs, old or not so old, had the word "hat" in them.

Jeb sighed and turned to inspect his side of the street. Behind him was a broken plate glass window with no indication of what the store might ever have been. Next to it was a bank; its named carved in the stone a few feet above Jeb's head. "Bank" was another word he knew by sight. "Bank, bank," he mumbled, "can't recollect no bank."

With his free hand, he reached behind him, fumbling until he found his hip pocket, pulled out a bathwater-gray handkerchief and wiped his face. Then he ran the cotton cloth over the top of his head.

"I sho' could use me a drink of that ol' fountain's water right about now," he said.

Jeb smacked his full lips at the remembered taste of the fountain's water. Pure. Not like the tinny taste at the retirement center. Pure and cold. The fountain's water had always been cold, regardless if the thermometer read a hundred and ten degrees or forty degrees.

He puffed toward the sign he couldn't see. None of the words looked familiar. Nor did any of the faded lettering partially covered by the sign. He stopped on the corner and looked behind him. The young black man had returned for another cigarette. Jeb stretched his arm to grasp a light pole for support, leaning into it to take some of the pressure off his knees. He looked up and down 172nd Street.

Jeb turned and faced the direction from which he had come. He bent and rubbed his knees. Straightening, he looked backward over his shoulder, across 172nd and up 173rd. Then back toward the bus stop. He looked in both directions repeatedly before finally reaching into his trousers for his lucky quarter.

Mr. Jeffrey had given him the quarter the first time he had taken Jeb cooning with him, and Jeb's old bluetick had treed three coons that night. "You sure trained him right," Mr. Jeffrey had said, grinning wildly and placing the newly minted coin into the little boy's hand.

Jeb held the quarter flat in the palm of his wrinkled hand.

"Okay," he said, "heads, thata way." He jerked his head back toward 173rd and beyond. "Tails, thisa way." He nodded toward the bus stop.

Jeb tossed the coin haphazardly in the air. As it fell, he could see himself and Roland, sitting on the fountain's edge, tossing the coin high into the air. He wanted to enlist in the Army when America joined the fight against the Germans in 1917, and Roland had tried to put the fear of the Lord in him.

"Niggers ain't good fo' nothin' in the Army 'cept fo' cookin' and cleanin' up afta white boys," Roland had kept telling him. "And besides. You is only fou'teen; they ain't agonna let you join no army."

"I's could lie. I's awfully big fo' fou'teen."

Roland took in the five-foot-nine frame and the massive arms. "I's don' know."

"I's tired of hoeing cotton," Jeb had countered. "I wants me an adventure."

"Cotton ain't gonna shoot you ass off," Roland said, shaking his head. "Ifn' I was you, I wouldn't be in no damn hurry."

Jeb had let the coin decide. And when he came home in 1919, he let the coin decide if he should ask Annabelle to marry him. Heads, yes; tails, no.

He grabbed the quarter as it fell to crotch level and slapped it on his left forearm. Before lifting his hand, he brought his arm closer to his face and peered into the dark recess of his cupped palm. Tails.

Shit, he thought, mighta knowed.

Jeb retraced his steps, stopped to rest briefly against the bus stop bench, and wiped away the sweat. At the corner, he looked up and down 171st Street before crossing. He chuckled. In the old days, the days before his legs bent, he would have plunged headlong across the street, pushing a wildly waving rack of women's dresses. He shuffled past the row of boarded up windows, looking up at the signs dangling from the storefronts, not recognizing any of the words.

He was at the end of the block before he remembered that Curran's Hat Company never had a sign that hung away from the building. He moved to the edge of the sidewalk and drug his legs back the way he had come, scrutinizing the bleached lettering on the buildings' façade for any familiar word.

When he arrived back at the corner, water began to sprinkle his head and shoulders.

Shit, I'd reckoned I'd be back home by now, he thought. But leas' I was right; I tol' that fool it was goin' t' rain.

As the drops increased in size and frequency, Jeb pulled his windbreaker over his head and began to look for more appropriate cover. All of the doorways were either boarded up or had iron bars stretched across them. He stuck close to the buildings as much for support as for shelter.

The building was long and, at the end, Jeb turned down the narrow alley. He saw a long row of crumbling tenement houses that had once sheltered the low-paid workers of the district--the seamstresses, the cutters, the runners.

Annabelle and I lived in a place like this, he remembered.

He and Annabelle had had three rooms on the top floor of a six-story building. When the weather was warm, they would sit on the wooden steps, he in his undershirt and work pants, and she in a thin cotton nightgown, and sip ice tea. They would talk and laugh and, once, he had made love to her there, her laughing and trying to pull her gown down over her bare buttocks, him with his britches stretched tightly between his knees.

From the back, the houses hadn't changed all that much. Little patches of yard not big enough for more than three tomato plants. Wooden staircases that once zigzagged from the sixth, sometimes seventh, floor to the top of the windows on the first floor now were missing some steps or the handrail had fallen off. On one of the buildings, the entire structure below the fifth floor had fallen away, leaving a wooden step dangling in mid-air. Laundry hung from open windows.

Jeb had never let Annabelle hang the wash on the sills. At least not until after the first four children had arrived. It looked trashy. Just because they were niggers, they didn't have to be trashy. Miss Molly had taught him that.

He tried to look up at buildings, hoping to see the Curran's Hat Company sign, but the driving rain kept him huddled beneath his jacket. Jeb picked his way disgustedly through the alley, strewn with old tires, broken bottles and ripped-open garbage bags.

He reached the end of the alley and looked up and down 170th. It looked exactly like 171st and 172nd. "Hell's bells," he muttered. Turning, he headed back to the bus stop.

Later that night, as Jeb sat on the edge of his narrow bed, he took the folded picture from his jacket pocket and opened it, smoothing the creases with his fingertips.

"I gots to find it, Sweet Petunia," he told Annabelle's picture, sitting on the bedside table. "But I ain't rememberin' where it's at." He laid back on the thin, floral spread and folded his hands, praylike, below his ribcage, the photo resting on his chest.

Close to midnight, Jeb woke to thunder and lightening bouncing around the room. He climbed stiffly out of bed and made his way to the tiny bathroom. As the urine passed from his body in short spurts, his head hung on his chest. He absently rubbed his left shoulder.

Jeb hobbled back to his bedroom. The word "Beaumont" popped into his mind as he pulled the covers over him.

That's right, he thought. We's used to live on Beaumont Street. And the fountain was two blocks from our house, right behind Curran's. "Thanks Sweet Petunia," he mumbled to Annabelle's picture. "I knews you'd help me 'member." He blew a kiss toward the cracked photograph and turned to face the wall.

Sunday dawned as gray and humid as Saturday. Jeb dressed and walked unsteadily down the retirement center's long hallway to the nurse's office. Nurse Gimble would write "Beaumont" for him. He poked his head in the doorway. The weekend attendant, a young man of about twenty, sat behind Nurse Gimbel's desk.

"Whattya need old man?"

Jeb stared at a point above the male attendant's left ear

"Well, out with it. Whattya want?"

Jeb fingered the piece of paper and pencil in his pocket.

"I haven't got all day."

"I's wanted to chat with Nurse Gimbel."

"Well, she isn't here, and I don't have time to 'chat.'"

Jeb stood in the doorway, still fingering the pencil and paper. "When she gonna be back?"

The attendant heaved a big sigh and looked up again. "Tomorrow, okay. Now go away. I'm busy."

Jeb turned and headed back to his room. As he passed the dining room, he stopped and watched Mrs. Greenley spoon oatmeal into her mouth. He poked his head further into the room, hoping that someone else might also be enjoying an early breakfast. "Shit," he muttered when he could see that none of the other tables were occupied. He took the pencil and paper from his pocket and stared at it, then at Mrs. Greenley, then back at the items in his hands.

He and Mrs. Greenley weren't exactly enemies, but they were a long way from being friends. The tantrum she had thrown and the foul things she had said when she first discovered that her room was next to Jeb's room still smarted. Since that day, more than three years ago, Jeb had tried to be polite to the ninety-year-old spitfire, but she had ignored him.

Jeb sucked in his breath and headed for Mrs. Greenley's table. When he reached his destination, he stood beside her chair, rubbing his left shoulder.

Mrs. Greenley ignored him and continued to scrape her spoon against the ceramic bowl.

Jeb coughed slightly. "'Scuse me, Missus Greenley," he said softly.

No response.

He fidgeted with the zipper on his jacket. "I's needs a great big favor."

The scraping spoon got louder.

"I's don' like to be askin', but I gots to."

Mrs. Greenley sat back in her chair and belched loudly. "I don't do favors for niggers."

Jeb looked around the dining room. Running water came from the direction of the kitchen. "You see," he said finally, "I never did learn to writ---"

"Well, of course not! You're a nigger. Niggers don't need to learn to write. Only stirs 'em up."

"Yesum. Yous got a point, Missus Greenley, but that's why I's needs you to---"

"I used to have the most beautiful handwriting in Atlanta. I won a contest once because of my beautiful handwriting."

"Thats mighty nice."

Jeb stared at the floor while Mrs. Greenley stared at her own memories. After a bit, he sucked in his breath. "Missus Greenley, I needs you to write the word 'Beaumont' on this here piece of paper fo' me." He thrust the paper at her.

She ignored it and stared down to her hands, once smooth, pink, and graceful, now gnarled and mottled with age spots, thin purple veins running helter skelter.

Jeb waved the paper.

Mrs. Greenley's green eyes darted toward Jeb. "Why you uppity–"

Jeb could feel his limbs start to tremble, "I's sorry, Missus Greenley, but, please." He heard the quake in his voice and felt the bile rise in his stomach. "I needs you to---"

Mrs. Greenley's round eyes narrowed. "Whatcha ya want it for?"

"I's, uh, I's, I's---"

"Well, out with it boy."

Jeb's head hung low as he scrunched his shoulders.

Mrs. Greenley grabbed the paper from Jeb's shaking, outstretched hand. "Oh, alright. This one time. Do you hear me, boy?"

Jeb swallowed. Hard.

"Only thing worse than a nigger is a whiny, sniveling nigger," Mrs. Greenley complained as she wrote on the paper.

Jeb chewed on his lower lip.

When she finished, she threw the paper at him.

He snatched at the floating paper, but missed. He grunted as he leaned over to retrieve it from the floor, then turned and shuffled from the room.

Mrs. Greenley's yelled across the room. "Don't bother me no more, boy. You hear me? You hear? You better mind me, boy."

As he reached the doorway, he stuck the paper in his pocket. Lumbering down the hallway, he could still hear Mrs. Greenley bellowing.

"You ungrateful nigger! Not even a 'thank you ma'am.' What's this world coming to when niggers don't know their place anymore?"

Not many buses ran on Sunday, and Jeb had to wait nearly two hours for one that would take him to the South Side. When he arrived at the corner of Peachtree and 171st, it was almost noon. The sky had cleared and the heat and humidity had risen rapidly. He eased his way off the bus and rested again on the concrete bench. While he sat there, the young black man across the street slipped from behind the iron-barred door and walked away.

Jeb ambled east on 171st. While he made his way down the street, he kept looking at the faded lettering for the word "hat" on the sides of the building. When he reached the corner, he took the paper on which Mrs. Greenley had written "Beaumont" from his pocket and compared it to the street sign, but none of the letters matched.

He trudged another block. Still no sign of "hat" on the buildings. At the corner, he again tried to match the letters on the street sign with the ones written on the paper. Nothing.

At the next block, the street sign was missing. His eyes searched the buildings for letters that looked like the ones on the paper. He saw a sign that had a "BE" as the first two letters, but the rest of the lettering had been graffited over.

Jeb labored on for another block, dragging his hand along the building's jagged bricks to help him keep his balance. He stopped every few minutes to catch his breath. When he reached the opposite corner, he leaned against lamppost.

I shoulda done run into those houses by now, he thought.

As he rested, he looked around. The buildings catty-cornered from him weren't buildings at all. They were piles of rubble with blackened frontages and collapsed roofs. Directly across from him, the corner lot was bare and littered with garbage. To his left, the corner building's side had caved in, strewing bricks and mortar into the street, causing the rest of the block's buildings to lean precariously to the right.

Jeb leaned heavier into the lamppost and massaged his knees. He closed his eyes and tried to remember where Beaumont was. Nothing came.

I gots to find it, he thought, them ol' bulldozers mos' likely be here tomorrowy.

Pushing himself off the lamppost, Jeb started across the street. When he reached the middle, he stopped.

"No," he said, "no, I's gots to be goin' the wrong way."

He looked in both directions, then down at his feet and rubbed his chin. He looked in both directions again and began to search his pocket for his lucky quarter.

Don' need it, he remembered. I's still on that street in the picture. Now let me think. Yesterday I went thata way.

Turning, Jeb cut across the street. He doddered more slowly along the crumbling sidewalk, leaning heavier into the building and pausing more often to wipe away the sweat. He reached 172nd. On the other side, the buildings gave way to the tenement houses. Smiling, he shook his head.

Jeb plodded along the street. From the front, the row of tenement houses he had seen yesterday looked as broken-down as they did from the rear. Steps were missing or had reverted into piles of concrete stones, paint hung in loose strips, windows were gapping holes, and in some places, entire sections of boards were missing from different parts of the structure. He made his way into the middle of the next block. He turned, his drawn eyebrows forming a heavy furrow in his forehead, and surveyed the area.

Now, ifn's I could only 'member which one was ours, he thought.

He shook his head. Nothing. He looked behind him and noticed his lengthening shadow. "Getting' late," he mumbled. "What's I gonna do? I gots to the find the fountain 'fo they tears down everything." He sighed and looked around one more time. "Well, I can'ts find it in the dark; I mights as well go on home."

Jeb turned and headed back the way he had come. It took twice as long to reach the bus stop. When he arrived, he sat heavily on the concrete bench. Darkness began to settle around him, softening the harshness of deteriorating area.

Looks kinda like it used to, he thought. I's wonders hows long I's gonna have t' wait fo' that bus.

He closed his eyes and let the night settle around him. While he slept, memories of Annabelle and the fountain floated through his dreams.

Annabelle sat daintily on the fountain's edge, her skirt pulled up to show long, shapely legs, shoes dangling from her hand. She swiveled and plopped her feet into the water, throwing her head back and laughing. Jeb had been so busy looking at her legs that he almost forgotten why he had brought her there. He pulled the ring box from his pocket, swung around and stuck his feet, shoes still on, next to Annabelle's. Her husky laughter got louder. She leaned so hard against him that he dropped the box into the pool. Laughing harder, she watched him flounder in the water, dressed in his best, and only, suit, trying to grab the floating black box.

The dream shifted to the two of them, walking hand-in-hand from their top floor apartment to the fountain, Annabelle heavy with the first of fifteen children. He had bathed her swollen legs in the water. Together they had made grandiose plans for the child Jeb was positive was a son and Annabelle was certain was a daughter.

The dreams became fragmented. Children splashing in the water. Miss Molly soaking her linen handkerchief in the water and dabbing at her long, slender, neck. Jelly sandwiches eaten during lunch breaks with Annabelle smiling by his side. Mr. Jeffrey slumped against the fountain's base, blood pouring from the wound in his chest, apologizing for not stopping the Klan for lynching Jeb's daddy.

Jeb's head jerked with a start. Opening his eyes, he could see that he was still at the bus stop and the sun was starting to rise.

"I gots t' get goin'," he said. "They's be here soon."

He inched his way up from the bench. His knees were stiffer than usual and more swollen from sitting up all night. He made the four block trek east, dragging his legs. When he reached the street that had the vacant corner, he turned south and headed toward the tenement houses. He shuffled past the row of derelict buildings and into the next block.

Reaching the center of the block, Jeb turned slowly in a circle, examining the decaying dwellings. Nothing looked familiar.

"I gots t' recognize somethin'," he said.

Jeb turned in another slow circle. He shook his head and hobbled toward the next block. As he crossed the street, signs of life began to appear. Several ancient and battered cars were parked in front of slightly less decaying buildings. A radio blared through one of the windows. A

German Shepherd on a short string barked weakly from a concrete stoop as he passed by. "I ain'ts gonna hurt you none," he said to the protesting animal. "I gots t' find Miss Molly's fountain, and I gots t' find it right away."

As he crossed into the next block, Jeb could see two people sitting on some steps about halfway down. He tried to move faster, but his swollen joints refused. When he finally reached the couple, Jeb recognized the baseball cap and the young black man beneath it. He had his arm around a skinny black girl, nibbling at her ear.

The young black man stopped and turned toward Jeb. "What's up, old man?"

"I's needs yo' help."

The young black man looked Jeb up and down several times before replying. "I'm busy." He turned the back to the woman and began to run his tongue along her neck. He stopped and looked back at Jeb. "What's in it fo' me?"

Jeb started toward the couple, reaching into his pocket for the newspaper clipping and the piece of paper Mrs. Greenley had written "Beaumont" on. "I needs some help." Jeb began to pull his hand from his pocket. "Please. I gots t' find this fountain."

The young black man sighed and took the clipping from Jeb's outstretched hand.

"It's on Beaumont, but I can'ts find Beaumont," Jeb said.

The young black man studied the picture, then shrugged his shoulders. "I hates to be the one to tell you this, ol' man, but them bulldozers started plowin' there last Thursday."

Jeb's mouth dropped open. "But it say next week. She say it say next week."

"This here picture is two weeks ol'," the young black man said. "See this here date." He pointed to the date in the top right hand corner.

Without realizing it, Jeb lowered his voice. "I gots t' find the family treasure."

The young black man cocked his head. "What?"

Jeb repeated himself louder.

"Ain't no such thing as a buried treasure. Not in this neighborhood anyways. Who you tryin' t' fool, you crazy ol' coot." The young black man looked Jeb up and down. "Whatcha looking fo'?"

"It's in the cobblestones. Please tells me. I gots t' find it."

The young black man stared at Jeb for a long minute, then pushed the girl aside and stood up. The crotch of his jeans drooped to his knees. He bounded down the steps. "C'mon, ol' man. I'll take you there." He pointed over Jeb's shoulder. "Beaumont's the street behind you."

The street without a sign.

The young black man jumped off the steps and pulled Jeb by the arm. "Let's go, ol' man. We gonna be rich!"

Jeb walked as fast as he could beside the young black man. As they walked one block to the south, Jeb told him the fountain's history. When they turned west, the landscape changed dramatically. The old houses had been demolished; piles of lumber and brick were scattered around. A wrecking ball hung quietly from its heavy chain. Heavy earth-moving equipment stood like silent sentinels over the small bulldozers and dump trucks. It was still quiet; the construction crew hadn't yet arrived. As they rounded a corner, Jeb stopped. "Miss Molly's fountain," he whispered.

The fountain had been almost cut in half by the bulldozers. Most of the cobblestones lay in a heap to the left. As they got closer and closer, Jeb could see the fountain's boy lying on its side, its sheared shoulder to the ground.

He moved as quickly as he could to the fountain's remains. Kneeling by the boy's face, he began digging at the loosened cobblestones with his hands.

The young black man dropped to his knees beside Jeb. "Is this where it's at?"

Jeb pried the bricks from their pattern and scratched at the red clay beneath them. Soon, his fingers struck something stiff and smooth. He gently wiped the clay away and removed the hardened leather pouch. He began to unwrap the rawhide strips.

"Gimme that," the young black man said and grabbed the pouch from Jeb's hands. "Yous too slow."

Jeb watched as he ripped the pouch open and pulled out several cracked and fading pictures, bits of yellowed paper and a black ladies comb. "What the fuck is up with this shit?"

Jeb reached for the objects.

The young black man shoved his face into Jeb's. "I thought you said this was a treasure, old man. This ain't nothing but useless bullshit." He flung the pouch's contents to the ground and jumped up.

Jeb scrambled to pick up the brittle pieces of his family history. He could feel the young black man pacing behind him, muttering obscenities.

The blurred tintype was his great-grandparents standing in front of their slave quarters, taken by Matthew Brady two hours before Sherman burned everything on the plantation.

Jeb gently laid the photo on the ground and held up the other two photographs. One was of his grandparents standing in front of the fountain; the other was of the mule Granddaddy inherited from Great-Granddaddy. The mule and the forty acres they lived on were the first things any Larson had ever owned outright. Then he picked up the scraps of paper. He didn't know what the pale scratches said, but Granddaddy had said that it was birth, death, and sale records of the Larson's and all the other slaves on the Winchester plantation. He stretched his hand toward the black comb that had been Great-Grandmama's, but he was jerked upright.

The young black man thrust a snarling face into Jeb's. "This it, old man? This all you got?"

The scraps of paper began to blow away.

Jeb looked down at the hand that was roughly clasped around his forearm. Scabby sores ran up and down the young man's arm and almost covered the soft inside if his elbow. "I's never said it was val'uble. I jest said it was my family's treasure."

"I can't fucking believe this!" The young black man jerked Jeb's arm again. "I ain't leaving here empty handed." He hauled Jeb to his feet and tried to put his hands in Jeb's pockets. "You got any money on you?"

"Alln's I gots is bus fare."

The young black man pushed Jeb back down on the ground. "You ol' motherfucker. Get it out!"

While Jeb fished in his pockets for the coins, the young black man kicked at the heaped pile of rubble. When Jeb pulled his hand out of his pocket, fifty cents lay in his palm. He looked at the young black man's twisted face then back to the change. He slipped his lucky quarter into his other hand and lifted his palm.

The young black man turned around. "Fifty cents! That's it! Fuck! Fuck you!" He slapped Jeb's hand away. The two quarters clanked as they hit the cobblestones.

Jeb bent back over his treasures. He scooped up the bits of paper and the photos and held them tightly against his chest.

The young black man reached down into the pile of Georgia-red clay stones and picked up the largest one. He slammed the brick against the back of Jeb's head, sending him sprawling across the ground.

"Fifty lousy fucking cents," the young black man yelled again as he smashed the brick against Jeb's head a second time. "Fifty mother-fucking cents ain't gonna get me outta this fucking neighborhood!"

Blood gushed from Jeb's skull.

"Fifty fucking cents," he muttered, picked up the quarters from the pool of blood and stalked away.

Jeb groaned and opened his eyes. The fountain boy's face stared back at him, his small mouth curved delicately into a smile.

"The family treasure," he said faintly. He pulled his weathered, withered hand from beneath his body, still clutching the paper and pictures.

He tried to look at them, but his eyes blurred. He brought them closer to his face, but the light was fading.

"Come on home," a voice said.

Jeb looked at the fountain boy.

That's Mama voice, he thought. Like when she used to call me in from playin'.

"Come on home," the statue repeated. "It's time."

"Time," uttered Jeb as his hand loosened on his treasures. Wind lifted the edges of the papers. "I gets t' go home now."

Heart Hunter

Robert couldn't sleep. Lying on Peggy's side of the bed, he watched the clock tick off the minutes. He rolled onto his back and stretched his arm across the bed. His fingers traced the sag in the mattress which Peggy's body had left. Robert grabbed her pillow hugged it to his chest, closing his eyes.

He ran his tongue over his lips, remembering the saltiness of Peggy's skin. He moved his tongue over his teeth, slowly tracing them and felt, not the broken crookedness of his own, but Peggy's small even ones. He buried his face in the pillow. A faint whiff of gardenias wafted from the goose feathers. Robert felt himself slip inside Peggy's warm softness, her soft panting a delicate sigh against his ear. The pillow muffled his low moan. Suddenly he threw the pillow across the room, groaned and rolled onto his stomach.

After a few minutes, Robert retrieved the pillow from the floor. He lay back down but immediately got up. He padded into the family room and paced for several minutes before stopping in front of the bay window. He leaned his forehead against the warm pane and watched the floating headlights of a car on the nearby highway.

"You sit there too much," his daughter had said in a phone conversation earlier that day, a conversation that had sounded exactly like the one he had with his son yesterday. "You need to get out more.

It's time. Mom's been dead two years. You promised her you wouldn't mope around like this. You don't want to spend the rest of your life alone, do you? You'll have to start dating sooner or later."

"Sixty-five's too old to start *dating*," he had told them. "It's been forty-five, no fifty-five, years since I've asked anybody but your mother for a date. I wouldn't know what to do. And besides," he had added, "do you think I'm going to live forever?"

Robert massaged the bridge of his nose. I don't even know how, he thought. What would I say? Who would even go out with an old fart like me?

When he looked in the mirror, Robert thought he looked old. Peggy had always told him that he looked twenty years younger, but lately he had begun to wonder if she had been lying. The lines around his emerald eyes were much deeper and always seemed to be present, even when he wasn't laughing, which was most of the time now. Heavy creases descended from his slightly-crooked nose to his square chin. He was sure they hadn't been there last year. Robert was thankful he still had all his hair, though it had turned from dusty brown to moonglow white. The small paunch that had developed after his sixtieth birthday had surprised him. He complained about it so much that his daughter gave him a treadmill for Christmas last year. He used it occasionally, but more often than not, it functioned as a clothes rack.

Turning back to the empty room, Robert picked up a picture of Peggy at their thirty-fifth anniversary party. She was laughing; one of the last times she had laughed easily before she had been diagnosed with breast cancer. He stared down into large, doe-brown eyes. "You promised," she seemed to say to him. "Remember? You promised you wouldn't cry forever." A work-roughened finger with fine graying hairs at the knuckle traced her smile.

"Okay. Okay," he said. "I'll give it a try. But I'm not going to bingo!"

Robert thumbed through the pile of newspapers on the floor beside his recliner and pulled out the weekly entertainment guide. He perched his glasses on the end of his nose and kicked back. Now, he thought, where does a guy go to meet women these days?

Robert did go out. Occasionally. He'd been to a few bars with some old friends from the bank but hated the blue-haze halo hanging inches above everyone's head. Peggy had been allergic to cigarette smoke, and he, too, had developed an intolerance for the toxic fumes. Going to the movies had helped ease his loneliness. Some. Once he tried to strike up a conversation with a woman who was also at the theater alone, but ended up only making a weak comment about the plot.

The tiny ad for the singles dance was in the lower left corner on page three. Perfect, he thought. He and Peggy had loved to dance. The jitterbug had been their specialty. Before the kids came along, they went dancing three or four times a week. After that, they had settled for being the sensation at all of St. Francis' dances.

Great band, he thought. The Will Keeler Brass was a group of ten middle-aged men who played everything from the '30s to the '90s. Robert remembered them from several of St. Francis' New Year's Eve parties and from some of his friends' kids' wedding receptions. And it's at the Regal Hilton. That oughta keep the riff-raff away. The Regal Hilton was located on the southern outskirts of Jefferson.

Robert rubbed the stubble on his chin. Hmmm, he thought, I wonder if the cleaners can get that spaghetti stain out of my tie.

***

"That'll be seven dollars," said the middle-aged woman wearing a platinum blue-sequined gown sitting behind the welcoming table. Bright blue eyeshadow and a black line running beneath her eyelid met at a point near her temple. Her heavy perfume reminded Robert of the stale air in a long-closed room. He peeled off seven one-dollar bills and turned away.

Tucking his wallet into the hip pocket of his gray knit slacks, he looked around the hotel's small, elegantly furnished lobby. Clusters of three and four women were scattered around the room. He nodded to a woman in a long black skirt who was staring at him. Robert ran his hand through his hair and adjusted the red silk handkerchief peeping above the pocket of his navy blue sports jacket.

"Gotta stamp your hand, honey," the middle-aged woman said.

He stuck out his fist and watched her stamp it with green ink.

"That's so stupid," Peggy would have said. "All you have to do is say you came out of the bathroom and the ink came off when you washed your hands. Who could argue with that?"

Robert pulled his hand away, bumping into a woman with bleached-blond hair and black roots who stood behind him. "Sorry," he said and backed away.

"You're looking fine tonight," she said.

"Uh, thanks." He ducked his head and moved around her. Robert was sure he heard her purring. He watched her out of the corner of his eye. He grunted and slipped inside the ballroom's double doors.

The band was playing a loud, unfamiliar tune. He sure missed Benny Goodman and Glenn Miller. That, in his humble opinion, was music. The room was almost a third full and dark compared to the lobby. A spotlight showered the band and lent a phosphorescent glow to their white tuxedos. The dance floor was crowded with people gyrating in a variety of moves.

What's that all about, he wondered, watching the guy who held one hand straight up in the air and the other wrapped around his partner's neck in a headlock. Robert shook his head and moved to the side while his eyes adjusted to the new darkness.

To his left and in front of the bar, women milled around. Some inspected the men who walked by; others swayed to the beat. One woman in a tight, low-cut, orange dress was thrusting her cleavage into some guy's face as he tried to light her cigarette. The guy's hands were shaking. Robert smiled a lopsided-smile.

"Hussy," Peggy would have whispered in his ear.

"Ah, you're jealous you don't have that much to show off," he would have whispered back.

"I've never heard you complain," she would have retorted.

He would have grinned. "Would it do any good?"

She would have playfully slapped him on the arm.

Robert moved out of the door's shadow and headed for the bar. He could feel eyes traveling over every inch of his 5'9" frame as he walked through the group of women. Some looked away as he passed by, but others kept staring with an "I need a man TONIGHT" look written boldly across their powdered faces. Ordering a beer, he stood in front of the bar.

His eyes swept over the crowd. He was surprised at the number of young people. Young as in thirty-five to forty. And at the number of women--out-numbering the men three to one. He spotted two women who looked to be about his age sitting near the bandstand. Well, he thought, maybe one of them will dance with me.

Spying an empty table in the corner farthest from the band, Robert headed for it. You're here to have some fun, he told himself. It's a lark. Get the kids off my back. He smiled as the band started playing "My Girl." It was one of Peggy's favorites. Enjoy the music, he thought. Have a couple of beers, listen to the music, maybe ask one of those ladies to dance, then leave.

"Would you like to dance?"

"Huh?" He turned and looked over his shoulder at a woman with long wheat-gold blond hair. She wore a frilly, pale blue dress one size too small.

"Would you like to dance?

"Well, uh, I, a, sure. Why not." Jeez, he thought, she must be desperate if she's doing the asking.

As they made their way to the dance floor, the band switched to "Dream Lover." Robert opened his arms. His body went stiff as she snuggled against him. Relax, he thought, it's a dance.

"Live around here?" Her voice wobbled; nervous.

"Excuse me?"

"What part of town do you live in?"

"City."

"Where?"

"The Meadows," he lied, giving the next neighborhood over.

"I live in Stoneybrook. Are you here with a singles group?"

"Uh, no. First time."

She tried to snuggle a little closer to him. The fragrance of pine needles drifted from her hair and reminded him of the stuff Peggy had used to clean the bathroom.

"What do you do?"

"Retired."

"From what?"

"Banking. I was vice president of First National's loan operations."

"What do you like to do?"

Robert looked down at the top of her head. A red dot the size of a pencil eraser glared from the middle of her white scalp. "Huh?"

"Any hobbies?"

Whatever happened to asking somebody their name before you asked their life history, he thought. "Oh, I spend a lot of time at the airport. I finished restoring a Cessna a couple of months ago."

"You're nuts!" Peggy had said when he mentioned buying the dilapidated little two-seater. "You don't even know how to fly a plane!"

"Not yet. But by the time I get it running, I'll have my license," he had said.

She had laughed when she went to see it. The engine leaked oil and wouldn't always turn over. Yellow foam burst from cracks in black vinyl seats. The red and white paint was faded and chipped. There were several nicks in the rusty propellers. "You're nuts!" she had managed to get out through the laughter.

The woman didn't reply.

"My name's Robert."

"Carol."

The music ended and they wound their way back to Robert's table. He nodded to the couple who had seated themselves on the opposite side of the ten-person table. Robert pulled out a chair and motioned for her to sit.

Carol ignored the gesture and turned to face him. "Do you jitterbug? I'm taking lessons and would love to be able to practice with someone *experienced*." The word "experienced" came out as a breathy sigh.

Robert's eyes widened; his eyebrows arched. "No. Not anymore," he said slowly shaking his head.

"Our newlywed couple wins," the loudspeakers shouted. "Eighteen hours and forty-two minutes. Let's give a big round of applause to the 1954 Arkansas Jitterbug Champs, Mr. and Mrs. Robert Sconfeltd."

"Well, maybe I'll ask you again," she said and drifted off through the crowd.

Well, maybe I'll say no, he thought, as he watched her hips sway. He nursed his beer and watched the women meander around the tables, looking the men up, down, and over like packages of bacon. Robert observed woman after woman approach man after man. When the two would head for the dance floor. When did the rules change, he wondered. Do women do all the asking now? Are they really like the women on TV? I'm too old for this. Maybe I shouldn't have come.

Will Keeler began talking to the crowd about the next song. "The Electric Slide" had a fast and rhythmic beat. The dancers lined up and were soon gliding and sliding across the floor. Robert watched the crowd and laughed. A short fat man in a red plaid shirt and black polyester slacks, which probably had an expandable waist, bumped into everyone around him. A young woman in a pink midriff blouse and blue jeans tripped over her feet. The woman in the orange dress he'd seen earlier was a good dancer. So was the woman in the cowboy boots and black leather skirt.

"'Cuse me." Robert looked up at the woman standing beside him. "Do you have the time?"

"Uh, no." He held up both wrists to indicate he wasn't wearing a watch. "Sorry."

"I was wondering what time it was."

"Oh."

She shifted from foot to foot. "Would you like to dance?"

"Can we wait till the next one? I don't care for line dances." He nodded toward the dance floor.

"Sure." She stood beside his chair and waited for the music to end. Robert pretended to watch the dancers. Out of the corner of his eye, he watched her move a lock of thick coffee-bean brown hair out of her eyes, smooth her dark green skirt, brush imaginary lint from her cream-colored blouse, twist the bracelet on her arm . . .

"It'll be a slow one next. Is that okay?" she said. Robert nodded that it was. "They always play a slow one after a fast one. Sometimes two, if it was a real fast one."

"Oh." He hadn't noticed the sequence.

The band switched to "Speak Softly Love."

"You've got to talk to your daughter," Peggy had said and plunked down on the couch beside him. "She wants that song from "The Godfather" played in the church."

"So? It's her wedding."

"But she can't," Peggy had blustered.

"Why not?"

"It's so. . .so. . .so. . .sexual. What will Father think?"

"I think Father knows she's going to have sex," he had whispered and leaned over to plant a kiss on her nose. Peggy's face had turned a pale red.

As Robert moved to stand up, the woman took his hand. Her pudgy fingers were sweaty and almost the same size as his. He wanted to pull away but didn't. Instead of heading directly to the dance floor, she led him through the maze of tables and people, winding up near the bandstand.

Robert put his arms around her. She tried to pull him closer, but again his body stiffened. Lighten up for God's sake, he told himself. Her hand got sweatier as they drifted around the dance floor. Peggy's fingers had been long and slim. Dry too. He wondered how much longer the music would last.

"Deep velvet nights, when we are one." The woman's voice was dry and husky in his ear. Her hand ran slowly from his waist to the nape of his neck and began a slow caress. he hairs on the back of his neck stood up. Oh my God, he thought. The dampness from her fingertips left a moist trail. Trying not to shudder, Robert stiffened his entire body. "Hold me warm against your heart." Her voice warbled and cracked on the last note.

Each time Robert tried to shift away from the body clinging to his like wet toilet paper, she shifted closer. Her blouse felt cheap and damp beneath his hand. Robert closed his eyes. Please, God, he thought, get this over with.

Let me have a coronary--anything-- help me out of here. I don't care what--
zap the electricity, give me appendicitis, a twisted knee, a kidney stone--a
big one--I don't care. Anything. Ple-e-a-se. Get me ou--"

"Let's stay for the next one," she whispered. Robert opened his eyes.
The music had stopped. "Okay? Please?"

He shrugged, unable to think of a good excuse why they shouldn't, and
stared at the floor as they stood among the other dancers.

"You're good looking," she said.

He pretended not to hear. The next number was a fast one. Thank God,
he thought, at least I don't have to touch her.

Robert wasn't good at free-style dancing and preferred dances that had
steps and a pattern, like the jitterbug, waltz, cha-cha or the foxtrot. Unlike
Peggy, whose arms dangled loosely by her sides, Robert never knew what to
do with his arms, so he used the old bend and tuck routine. Bend at the
elbow, tuck into the ribs, fingers ready to start snapping if the music was
right. If it wasn't, his hands hung there, swinging in mid-air. While Peggy
had gently swayed her hips and her right foot delicately pointed in ballerina-
style in front of her, Robert shuffled his size twelve's back and forth and let
his torso careen from side to side.

*"You look like a scarecrow on a windy day," Peggy had always teased.
Then she would laugh, a high tinkling sound.*

He had always shrugged and stuck his tongue out at her.

Robert's eyes moved slowly up from the dance floor, past his partner's
black high heels, up her nylon-less legs, over her skirt and blouse, which
was open at the throat, up her neckline, past her smiling lips and into her
hazel eyes. That was all it took. Suddenly she started twirling and twisting,
stopping briefly to point at the ceiling, then at the floor.

Oh shit! he thought, oh shit! Robert froze the muscles of his face into a
semi-smile. He tried to ease his way back into the crowd of dancers, but
they were moving back as well. First she pointed high in the air, then thrust
her breasts out, swung her hips to the right and pointed at the floor in the
opposite direction. When the music came to a halt, she pointed directly at
him, mouthing "You're mine tonight."

With the smile frozen on his face, Robert screamed so that only he could
hear. Now God, if I'm gonna die of a heart attack, let it be now. Please. Let
it be now.

She glided over to him; sweat running down her face.

Robert was bent over double, his hands on his knees and panting
heavily. "I gotta sit down," he said, "I'm not as young as I used to be. That's

quite a workout." Yeah, that'll work, he thought. Rivulets of water ran down her hand as she led him off the dance floor.

When they arrived back at the table, Robert motioned to the chair on his left. "Would you like to sit down?" Please say no, he thought.

"In a minute. Gotta go potty. I'll be right back."

Robert breathed a small sigh and sat down. Maybe she won't come back, he thought. He took a few fast gulps from his warm beer. He had been sitting there for several minutes when an accusing voice came from behind him.

"I didn't think you liked to fast dance."

"I never said that."

Carol plopped down in the chair on his right. "Are you gonna dance with *her* all night?"

"Uh, I don't--"

"Well, I've read all the books on relationships and I know what men want," she proclaimed.

"Oh?" Robert cupped his chin in his hand and cocked his head. This oughta be good he thought.

"They want someone who is going to be attentive, and--"

He didn't hear the rest of what she was saying. Over Carol's left shoulder, Sweaty Palms, as he had come to think of her, had returned and was making wild gestures. First she would point at Carol and give the ol' heave ho sign. Next she would point at herself, then him, and finally clasp her hands together like a boxer winning a prizefight.

"And they want someone who is going to--" Carol continued.

He tried to concentrate on what she was saying. Sweaty Palms made another heave-ho gesture. Robert ran his hand through his hair.

"And women have to be--"

Sweaty Palms squeezed between the chairs until she was behind Robert. "Dump her. She's a loser," she whispered in his ear. He shrugged again.

"Humph," said Carol. "If you want to talk to *her* all night, I'll leave the two of you alone." She flounced out of her chair and out of Robert's sight.

"That's better," said Sweaty Palms. She eased into the chair on his left. "Mind if I smoke?" She pulled a crinkled pack and matches from her pocket and lit one without waiting for him to stammer out a reply.

"What do you do?" she said.

"Retired, but I'm a pilot at heart. Got my license last month."

"FAN-tast-ic."

"How 'bout you?"

"Sales. Lots of money in sales, didya know that? What d'ya fly?"

"Cessna."

"FAN-tast-ic."

They sat in silence while the band announced it was taking a 15-minute break.

"I haven't seen you here before," she said.

"First time."

She leaned over and ran three fingers beneath the knit fabric of his tie. "Nice. I like the way the grey squares overlap the red circles."

"Thanks. It's my favorite."

"What are you drinking?"

Robert picked up the brown bottle in front of him and showed it to her.

"Now be nice," Peggy would have chided.

"Beer."

"Well, bless your little heart."

Robert looked at her, his eyebrows drawing together, trying to understand what that meant. She took a long draw from her cigarette. "That's FAN-tast-ic."

"My name's Robert."

"Michele. And think.I wasn't gonna come out tonight." She picked up Robert's hand from the table and held it between her two wet ones. "Your hands are cold."

"Yeah they are." He slid his hand out of her grasp.

"I was gonna stay home and watch TV, but then I wouldn't have met you." Her lips curled.

Robert didn't answer and stared at the tablecloth. Okay, he thought, now what do I say? He didn't want to be unmannerly, but he couldn't return what he felt might be a compliment.

"Let me tell you about myself," she said. "I'm single. No kids. And I have more money than I know what to do with." Her flashing eyes locked with his. Robert didn't say anything. "I gotta go get a drink. I'll be right back. Don't go anywhere."

How rude, he thought. She could have at least asked if I wanted another one. As soon as she was halfway across the room, Carol slid into the seat she had vacated a few minutes earlier.

"Well, it's about time," she said.

"Excuse me?"

"If you want to talk to *her* all night--"

"Look." His voice took on a harsh tone. "I came by myself, and I'll be leaving by myself. Who I talk with or dance with is nobody's business but mine."

"I meant that if you'd rather be alone with--"

"I came to meet new people. Maybe this--"

"Well, I've read all about relationships and I know--"

"Tell her to bug off," Sweaty Palms whispered in his ear.

Robert jumped. He hadn't seen Sweaty Palms come back to the table.

"You're mine," she whispered in his ear as she plopped into the seat on Robert's left.

The scent of pine needles mixing with the cloying aroma of musk perfume and cigarette smoke almost made Robert gag. He stared at the tablecloth. Holy hell, he thought, back in my day women acted like ladies in public. Running his hand along the tense muscles in his neck, he looked at Carol, on his right, who was rattling on about relationships, her father, and power tools. On his left Sweaty Palms kept whispering in his ear, "Dump her. You're FAN-tast-ic and you're mine. Tell that loser to take a hike."

As the band returned from its break, Robert looked up at the ceiling. He had an overwhelming desire to make the sign of the cross. "Thank you," he said silently. "Thank you."

"C'mon, let's dance," said Sweaty Palms. She grabbed Robert's hand with her damp one, dragging him out of his chair.

Carol glared at them. "Hey, I thought you weren't--"

Robert shrugged. Sweaty Palms again led him through the jam of chairs and people until they were near the bandstand. Then she turned and led him to the center of the crowded dance floor. The band swung into "A Groovy Kind of Love."

"What a stupid song," Peggy always said whenever it came on the radio.

Sweaty Palms wrapped her arms around Robert's neck and began to rotate her hips into his. He stood there, swaying his torso. He didn't want to encourage her, but he felt old familiar stirrings in his groin.

"You an' me, we gotta groovy kind of love," she sang. Her voice felt like sandpaper against his ear. She was off key, humming the tune when she didn't know the words.

Sweaty Palms unlocked her hands from Robert's neck. One hand glided to the side of his head and began to caress his earlobe. The other slid to his waist, stopping to finger a belt loop. Slowly her hand moved around his waist and dropped, cupping his left buttock. Her fingers splayed, pressing firmly into his flesh. Robert tried to push her away. Jesus H. Christ, he thought. Worried his half-erection would increase her ardor, Robert tried to push her away again. The hand massaging his ear dropped to his right buttock. Using both hands she gently pulled his hips into hers. He tried to push her away again. Shit, he thought, when did women start acting like whores in public?

"We got a gro-o-o-vy." Her voice faltered she tried to hit a high note. As the song ended, she lifted her head and planted a small kiss on Robert's chin.

He froze.

Sweaty Palms parted her lips in anticipation.

Robert placed both of his hands on her shoulders and pushed her away. "No," he said. "I'm sorry. . ."

"Aw, come on." She ran a blunt fingernail along his zipper. Robert closed his eyes and sucked in his breath.

"No. No. I can't." He turned and walked away.

Sweaty Palms stood in the middle of the dance floor, her mouth hanging open. She watched him elbow his way through the crowd and back to his table. Then she shoved through the dancers, moving with long, manly strides toward his table.

Robert ran his hand over his face and down along his neck. "Look, I'm sorry," he said as she stood in front of him with her feet spread apart, her hands on her hips and her chest heaving. "It's not that I--"

"Teaser," she hissed. "No good asshole."

"Maybe you're right. I probably shouldn't have come here. This was a bad idea. I'm sorry. Really. I'm sorry."

"No good asshole," she hissed again.

Robert's eyes narrowed. His jaw muscles tightened. "Look, I said--"

"Bastard." Sweaty Palms turned on her high heel and stomped away.

Robert picked up his empty beer bottle and played with it. Well, he thought. So much for dating.

"Wow, that was some scene." The husky voice drifted across the table.

Robert looked up. He hadn't noticed the woman with snow-cloud gray hair sitting across from him. He chuckled. "Yeah. It sure is a different world these days. My wife--" He stopped and looked away.

"Go on. Your wife?"

"I was going to say my wife would have never acted like that." He paused. "Or used that kind of language."

"Has she been gone long?"

Robert looked at her, his eyebrows drawing together.

"I'm sorry. You said 'would have.' I assumed--"

"Two years."

"I lost my husband last year. You must miss her a lot."

Robert shook his head slowly. "Yeah. My kids have been on my back about getting out more, so I thought I'd give this a try. Obviously not one of my better ideas."

The woman laughed. A deep throaty laugh. She scrunched up her face and, with a high pitch tone, mimicked her own children. "'You sit there too much. You need to get out more. You promised Dad that you wouldn't mope around like this.'" She paused and rolled her Easter-candy-blue eyes. "Mine too. So here I am."

Robert chuckled and stuck his hand across the table. "My name's Robert Sconfeltd."

The band began to play "String of Pearls."

She grasped his hand with her small, dainty one. "Finally! Some decent music! Louise Baker." She smiled, straight, even teeth showing. "Nice to meet you, Robert."

Robert's eyes crinkled; the lines deepened. He fingered the empty beer bottle and began to pick at the label. He smiled and rocked the beer bottle back and forth on the table. He ran a hand over his face and along the back of his neck. He looked at Louise. She was smiling. He ran a hand through his hair. He adjusted the cuffs of his starched white shirt. He played with the red silk handkerchief. He straightened his tie. He cleared his throat. "Say, Louise?"

She raised her eyebrows. "Yes?"

Robert cleared his throat again. "Wouldyouliketodance?"

Julie Failla Earhart

Sometimes You're the Bug;
Sometimes You're the Windshield

The Robbery

"Nobody move."

"Nobody move." The voice was louder and gruffer this time.

Cindy's head jerked to the right.   Inside the double glass doors stood a man; a man pointing a small gun in her direction. "Aw, jeez," she said. "Not again." Cindy stopped adding up the credit card receipts and rolled her black eyes.

Robberies happened here at the Truckers Rest Haven & Laundromat at least once a month. They came in, took the money and left. Nobody had ever fired their gun. Cindy often wondered if the guns were really loaded. You'd think the owners would get wise and hire some security people, thought Cindy. But no-o-o-o, that would make life too easy.

"Hear me. Nobody, nobody move. "He held the gun in both of his tobacco-stained hands like he had seen policemen do on TV. He waved it around a few times.

"Nobody move and nobody'll get hurt."

Why does he keep saying that Cindy wondered and tossed her honey-blonde ponytail over her left shoulder. Like who's gonna move besides me? What an idiot! Can't he see there isn't anyone here but me? Well, except Floyd, and everybody knows he doesn't count.

The man shifted the gun to his left hand and reached into the torn pocket of his red flannel shirt with his right. He inched over to the counter, his cracked brown cowboy boots scuffing along the linoleum. With a quick jerk, he flung a piece of brown paper into Cindy's face.

She threw up her hands to catch a paper sack.

"Fill it with all the green stuff," he said as low as he could. "And hurry up."

Okay, okay, thought Cindy, reaching a small hand into the cash drawer. Don't have a cow. Hmm, wonder if I should include those moldy sandwiches in the deli? She had been watching three tuna fish sandwiches turn from an emerald green to a deep Kelly green for almost a week. Science had always fascinated her. Nah, she decided, he probably wouldn't think it was funny.

The guy walked over to the far side to the counter where the pickle jar stood and looked around. Cindy watched him out of the corner of her eye as she put a handful of dollar bills into the sack. When he turned around, she tossed the bag toward him. "Definitely one of those bug days," she muttered.

"What? Shut up."

Cindy knew not to say anything. Give them the money and they'll leave.

Hurry up, she thought, my feet hurt. She leaned over the counter, cupping her hand in her chin. The clock over the beer cooler read 3:30 a.m. Cindy had been behind the counter since noon. Her luck Dorothy hadn't shown up for work. She didn't really mind pulling a double shift.

The guy with the gun was pacing back and forth in front of a rack of *Time* magazines.

What is he waiting for she asked herself. I've already given him the money. Why is he hanging around? What's with this guy? Cindy watched him pace up and down, the tail of his shirt flapping against a pair of jeans that were rolled up about six times around the ankles. He was muttering to himself but she couldn't make out what it was. Didn't care either.

The man stopped abruptly in front of the counter. He looked at her with blue-green eyes that reminded her of storm clouds during tornado season.

"You gotta come with me," he said.

Cindy gave him her famous "no way" look---blond eyebrows puckered together in the middle of her forehead, one corner of her mouth sucked in. It was known to put a stop to almost anything. "Why?"

"'Cause I don't want nobody identifying me to the cops."

"Hey, as far as I'm concerned you're wearing a mask. Who do you want to be Dracula? Frankenstein? Clinton?"

"Nope, ain't gonna buy it. You gotta come with me."

He started waving the gun again. Cindy sighed heavily.

"Look," she said, "I promise I won't say anything. Just get out of here and leave me alone."

He reached over the counter and grabbed the sleeve of her pink sweater. She stumbled as he pulled her forward.

"Okay, okay. I'm coming." Cindy smoothed her sweater, hopped onto the counter and swung her long denim-clad legs around almost hitting the guy in the head with the tip of her snake skin cowboy boots. "Sorry." Cindy smiled as pretty as she knew how.

"Yeah, sure let's go." He grabbed her arm again, pulling her off the counter and thrust the gun in her face. "Remember, I'm the boss. Do like I say."

"Okay," she said rolling her eyes. Definitely a bug day she thought shaking her head.

The guy pushed her towards the door and swung around like he heard someone coming up behind him.

"Save your energy. There isn't anybody here but me an' Floyd."

"Who's Floyd," he said, turning his head left and right.

Cindy pointed to the rear of the store. A white bird cage hung from the ceiling next to a display of motor oil. A brown hamster stood on its hind legs and peered at them, as if begging to go along.

"Oh."

"Take care of the store, Floyd," Cindy sang out.

"Come on," he said, nudging her with the gun.

They reached the door, and he actually held it open for her. Cindy looked at him in stunned silence. With a defiant tilt to her chin, she marched past him and into the cold night air. She turned and put her hands on her slim hips.

"Now what?"

"Don't you think you should lock up?"

Cindy gave him her no-way look again.

"O-o-o-okay. Maybe not. Stupid question."

Cindy began to tap her foot impatiently, hands still on her hips.

"This way." He pointed the gun to the right side of the building.

Cindy marched around the corner where a big rig stood; engine running, no lights. Well, it least oughta be warm in there she thought.

The man pushed her up into the cab and scampered around to the other side and clambered in. Settling himself in the driver's seat, he gunned the motor and ground the clutch. The truck lurched with a sudden start slamming Cindy against the door. "Better put your seat belt on. I'm not good at this," he said smiling shyly.

Oh great, an amateur thought Cindy, rolling her eyes again. Well, at least I don't have to stand up she thought and propped her boots on the dashboard.

The truck lurched and swayed along the outer road. He barely missed a red Volvo coming in the opposite direction.

"Where are we going?"

"Well, I gotta get this load of pigs to Nebraska before Monday morning.

Pigs! Nebraska! That was 1300 miles away. . . "Oh shit!" Cindy looked in the side-view mirror but couldn't make out any shapes in the dark. Funny, she thought, I don't smell anything. Aren't pigs supposed to stink?

They rode in silence for a while, the grinding of the gears began to give Cindy a headache. "Hey look. I gotta --."

Cindy and the guy jumped as the CB crackled into life. "Breaker one-nine. Hey good buddy, got your ears on. Ten-four."

"Can I get it," said Cindy, her voice rising. She had seen this on TV a million times and had always wanted to talk on a CB. She even had her handle picked out.

"Okay, but don't say nothing. I gotta gun, remember?" He groped down into his crotch but couldn't find the small pistol. Then he remembered he put it in his shirt pocket when he climbed aboard. How stupid he thought to himself.

"Hey good buddy," she whispered in her sexiest voice. "This is the Esmerelda Queen." Cindy thought it was sexiest name in the world. "What can I do for you," she purred. "Ten-four," she added quickly.

"Well hi there little lady. This here's the Rocket Man. Wanted to let you know your rear doors are a flapping. Sure hope it's an empty run. Ten-four."

"Damn," yelled the guy pounding the steering wheel with both hands.

Cindy dropped the microphone in her lap and put both hands over her mouth to keep from laughing out loud. What a doofus! "Problem?"

The guy whipped the truck off the road, jumped out and ran to the back of the truck. The rear left door was swinging back and forth. "Damn it. Where did those pigs go?" he screamed into the night air. Gravel flew in all directions as he kicked at the ground. He swung at the swaying door but missed and did a quick two-step to keep from falling.

Cindy watched the tantrum as she leaned against the rear of the truck, arms folded across her small chest. The guy turned his back to the swinging door and stood there, hands locked behind his neck. He lowered his arms and stomped the ground with his right foot. Cindy almost laughed out loud at the sight of a grown man acting like a four year old.

"Oh well," she yelled at his back. "Sometimes you're the bug, sometimes you're the windshield. Looks like you're having a bug day too."

Whirling, he stalked back toward the truck as if he hadn't heard her. "Get back in the damn truck." He kicked at the gravel again and ran to the front of the truck.

Cindy, still rocking with laughter, got in in time. He slammed it into reverse and started turning the wheel to make a U-turn. "It's one way," she said, biting her lower lip to keep from giggling. What a doofus, she thought again.

"Oh yeah," he growled. He had forgotten he had pulled onto I-89 a mile from the truck stop. They drove in silence for 10 miles before they came to the next exit ramp. He ignored the red light at the top of the ramp, and swung the truck so sharply Cindy could almostfeel its sides scraping the asphalt.

"Slow down. You're gonna kill us."

"Shut up. And look for those damn pigs."

"How many are we looking for?"

"Oh, about 75."

"You lost 75 pigs," squealed Cindy. She slapped both hands to her mouth again to keep from bursting out laughing. She turned toward the window and could see both their reflections in the streaked glass. He looked like he was gonna be sick.

"You okay?"

"Hell no. I lost a load of pigs. They're worth about $150,000. How do you think I feel?"

"Sorry." She studied his reflection in the window. Short brown hair. A bump on his straight nose. Pointy chin. Sideburns that needed trimming. Cindy felt sorry for the guy.

"What's your name?"

"David. My friends all call me "Davey.""

"Hi Davey.. My name is Cindy."

"Yeah, I know."

Cindy was surprised. He knows? Maybe this isn't so funny after all she thought. She started to squirm in the seat. Cindy squinted her eyes to get a better look at him in the headlights of on-coming cars. Well, maybe he looked a little familiar she thought. Tons of guys came through the truck stop e day but she never paid much attention to any of them. She pointed ahead to the exit sign that would lead them back to the truck stop. "Isn't this your exit?"

"Thanks."

"How long have you been driving a truck?"

Davey turned to glare at her. "A while."

"What's a while?"

"A while, okay. Give me a break."

Davey turned his eyes back to the road as a banana yellow volkswagen bug swerved into his lane. The air brakes squealed.

****

Davey's Story

Sometimes you're the bug, sometimes you're the windshield. That's my philosophy in life. I drive a truck. A big rig, ya know. I usually haul cattle between Dallas and Santa Fe but sometimes I haul other stuff. Once I hauled a load of turkeys to Oregon. I do okay at it. Driving that is. It's that my legs are kinda short and I can't reach the clutch unless I sit right. And I always grind the gears. Can't get the hang of it. I've been through three clutches in the last six months. Trucking isn't everything it's cracked up to be. Heck, most people think all I do is ride around, toot my horn, pick up girls, and drink beer. And cuss a lot. Don't forget the cussing. Truckers can cuss almost as good as sailors, or so they say.

Well, sure, I've picked up a lot of girls. Never had a problem there. All I have to do was say I'm a trucker and the girls almost drop their drawers right there. I can't figure it out for the life of me. I picked up VD a couple of times and a few months back, I got a real bad case of crabs from some red-haired woman with gigantic hooters in Amarillo. I never itched so bad in my life; thought I was gonna die. Sure wish I could remember her name.

Anyways, I kinda liked it that way until I met Cindy. She works the graveyard shift at the truck stop near Fort Worth. I do my best to stop in there when I know she'll be there. Once, I was late with a load, a first, to spend a few minutes with her. Cost me $300 but it was worth it.

Cindy is the prettiest thing I've ever seen; tall and thin with blond hair and the prettiest skin. I once bet $1000 it'd be real soft to touch, but she looked at me like I was nuts so I dropped it. And don't forget those huge black eyes. I wonder what those eyes looked like in starlight. And she's smart too. Knows all about football, baseball and diesel engines. She told me she could change the oil in the big rigs, if push came to shove. Her daddy taught her. He was a trucker too.

Cindy makes me feel real important and always seem glad to see me. No matter what, she stops doing whatever it is e time I walk in. And the smile that lights her face is brighter than sunshine any day of the week. She doesn't wear a wedding ring and I've never heard her mention another fella. So, maybe, I have a chance.

Once I stayed there all night; was going to ask her out, but never quite got up the nerve. I hung around all night. Must of drank a million cups of coffee.

I like watching her work. Her fingers are long and thin with pretty pink nails. She always wears her blond hair in a ponytail with a turquoise barrette. I think about Cindy a lot. Especially on those real lonesome stretches of highway. I wonder what she looks like in the morning, what she wears to bed, if she makes noises when she's makin' love, what color her toothbrush is. Betcha $50 it's green.

I'm not used to people being nice to me so I kinda shy away from them. That's why I like truckin' so much; even though I not good at it.

Anyways, that's besides the point. We were talking about Cindy. I have this great idea to get her to like me. Ya see, I gotta haul this load of pigs to Nebraska next week. So, I thought I could pretend to rob the truck stop. Be real serious and tough, ya know, and kidnap her and take her with me. And by the time we get back she'll be so in love with me that she'll marry me the next day. Great idea, huh?

****

The Wreck

The air brakes were squealing as Davey almost stood on the brake pedal. His knuckles were white from clenching the wheel and there was a white line around his mouth. The crunch and grind of metal could be heard beneath the screeching brakes.

"Ah-h-h-h-h-h-h-h-h-h-h-h." Cindy's head hit the side window, bursting it into a billion slivers of glass.

The truck stopped. Silence.

Cindy was lying sprawled across the blue vinyl seat.

Davey started breathing heavy in short, sharp snorts.

"You okay?"

"I-I-I-I think so. What about you?" he asked as he turned to face her.

One tiny speck of glass had cut Cindy right between the eyes and a drop of blood was slowly running down her nose. "I think so, too."

Davey scooted across the seat, and gently wiped away the blood. "I'm sorry. I didn't mean for you to get hurt."

Davey's door flung open. A teenager with flaming-red hair hanging past his shoulders and a t-shirt emblazoned with a skeleton and cross bones stood there. A dagger earring dangled from his nose. Davey didn't see much more than that before the guy hauled him out by the britches leg. "Hey, what'd ya think--" Before he could finish, the boy slammed Davey into the side of the truck, grabbed him by the collar and pushed him toward the wreckage.

"Look, look what you did to my bug," the boy screamed in Davey's ear. "Look what you did, you stupid idiot."

"Sorry, but it ain't my fault. You pulled in front of me."

"Like hell I did."

Cindy had crawled out of truck and was looking at the mangled yellow pile. She held a wad of paper napkins between her eyes to stop the bleeding. "Hey, look you big galute. It wasn't his fault. You cut him off."

"Shut up bitch. Say your prayers asshole," the boy said, drawing back his fist. Davey threw up his arms, ready to fight. He didn't like to fight, but never backed down from one.

Cindy ran over and started kicking the guy in the ankle. He swung around and hit her.

She sprawled on the ground. Blood ran from her nose and into her open mouth.

Davey's fist slammed into the boy's stomach.

****

Cindy's Story

Sometimes you're the bug, sometimes you're the windshield. That's my philosophy in life. I work at a truck stop. Have for almost a year now. I like it a lot. The boss says that I have the right attitude to keep those truckers in line.

They're not bad guys, the truckers. Most of 'em think they're Don Juan but I just laugh. I have no desire to hooked up with a man. Don't get me wrong, I like guys. It's that the divorce was really hard. Talk about feeling like a bug. I'm still not sure why Buck left me.

There I was, standing at the kitchen counter one afternoon making meatloaf and, wham. He comes in, packs his bags, says he wants a divorce and leaves. I didn't even have time to scrape the hamburger off my hands.

That's beside the point. The truckers like me, I can tell. They always stop for a little chit-chat after they've paid for their gas and munchies. I know a lot about baseball and football so we talk about that a lot. They were Buck's favorite sports. I'm real partial to Joe Montana. Isn't he the handsomest man in the world? My Buck looked a little like him. I have this daydream that I'll look up one day and Buck will be standing there. And I know what I'll do too. First I'll ask him why he left, then I'll kick him in the privates for hurting me so much.

Sorry about that. I was telling you about the truckers. One time this guy bet $1000 my face would be real soft to touch. I looked at him like this (she gives her "no way" look) and he dropped it---real quick. I bet the road gets real lonely, especially at night. So, I always try to act real happy to see them when they come in. I know how they feel. See, I live in a pop-up camper over behind the Amoco station. It's not too bad. Sure beats living in that trailer with all Buck's memories in it.

Anyways, let's get back to the point. It gets real lonely for me sometimes too. Then I'm glad they like to talk to me. But things'll get better. Heck, it could be worse. If I hadn't gotten this job I would've had to go back to Oklahoma. I guess you could say the bug isn't dead yet.

****

Cindy and Davey

"Davey, stop. You're killing him," screamed Cindy through a wad of bloody paper napkins.

His fist stopped in mid-air. "Aw, what the hell," Davey mumbled to himself and hit the boy one more time. He walked away, massaging his hand.

Cindy didn't mind when Davey first lit into the guy. He deserved it. She was shocked when he hit her. Nobody had ever hit her before. It hurt. A lot!

The boy lay against the crushed hood of the bug, gulping air. He didn't move. Blood spilled from a cut in his check and ran the off the side of his face, forming dark red pools against the banana yellow. A wailing siren could be heard in the distance.

"You okay,?" Cindy took the paper napkins from her nose. Most of the bleeding had stopped.

"Yeah, I'll be fine."

They walked back to the truck, the grey dawn beginning to spread across the sky.

The truck didn't seem to be damaged except where Cindy hit the window with her head.

A police car howled past them, screeched to a halt, backed up and parked beside the bug. A six-foot tall state policeman climbed out. "What's going on here?"

"A little accident officer," said Cindy.

"Little? Looks pretty big to me," said the officer.He took a small notebook out of his breast pocket and began to write.

"How did you know we were here, officer," asked Cindy in her sugar-coated voice.

"Nobody's had time to phone yet."

"Didn't. Another problem up the road. What happened here?"

The guy on the bug moaned and tried to raise his head. It fell back with a clunk against the hood.

The officer strode over to the boy. He looked at the guy and back to Davey who had started massaging his hand again. "Wanna tell me what's going on here."

Davey felt like a bug that had splattered against the windshield. It was over, he knew it. He didn't get Cindy to fall in love with him and now he was headed off for jail. "Shit," he muttered.

"Well officer, it was like this," said Cindy. "Me and Davey here dropped off a load sheep and are headed for Amarillo. We're supposed to pick up a load of cows in the morning and have them in Kansas City by Tuesday. Now, thanks to this bozo," she jerked her thumb toward the boy, "we're gonna be late."

"What about this guy?"

"Well officer --," Davey started.

"It was like this," interrupted Cindy, her black eyes twinkling mischievously. "This guy was standing next to this wreck waving and flapping his arms. We thought he might be hurt or something so we stopped. When we got out, he tried to rob us. Davey, what did you do with the gun he had?"

"Gun, what gun," he stared at her blankly. "Oh yeah, the gun." He pulled it out of his shirt pocket and handed it to the officer. "Here ya go, officer. Attempted robbery. That's what it was, attempted robbery."

Cindy nodded her head vigorously in agreement.

The officer glared at them before turning toward his car. He called for an ambulance and a tow truck. "I need you two to appear at the police station over in Monroe City tomorrow morning at 10 a.m."

"But officer --," Cindy started.

"Gotta get a statement. He," the officer jerked his head toward the bug "oughta be coming around by then."

"But officer --," yelled Cindy as he walked away.

"Be there," he said over his shoulder. "I gotta go. Some other idiot let about 100 pigs loose about 50 miles up the road." He shook his head as he climbed back into his patrol car.

Cindy and Davey looked at each other. They started laughing. And laughing. And laughing.

"Should we claim 'em?" asked Cindy.

"Oh, I don't know. Let's drive up there and see what's going on."

"Maybe we should wait for the ambulance," said Cindy as Davey brushed shredded glass from the vinyl seat.

"Nah. He'll be all right."

Davey turned the key; the diesel engine roared into life. As he pulled out onto the highway, the first ray of the rising sun glared on the windshield.

"Looks like this could be a windshield kind of day," Cindy said.

Stolen Identity

From the doorway of the bedroom, Lydia could see the full length of the doublewide trailer. She put her hands on her round hips and sighed contentedly. Everything's perfect, she thought.

Since 6 a.m., when her husband, Gene, left for the machine shop, she had been cleaning. The orange and yellow fingers of the shag carpet stood at attention, the recliner looked almost new since she'd re-stuffed and sewn the torn arm and the chrome on the kitchen appliances reflected the fluorescent light.

The late afternoon sun waned across the round table and four chairs cramped in the bay window, the carefully arranged china, silverware and dull glow of the wine glasses. She had even taken the pile of magazines heaped up beside Gene's recliner and her end of the brown-and-yellow-plaid couch and placed them in neat rows on the coffee table. *American Hunter, Sports Illustrated* and *Playboy* on the left; *Ladies Home Journal, Country Living,* and *Redbook* on the right.

Lydia smiled as she realized that the placement of the magazines reflected their sleeping positions—he on the left, she on the right.

Closing her eyes, she took a deep breath, pulling in a mixture of the pine- and lemon-scented cleanliness of the trailer and the lasagna baking in the oven. She stood there for almost a full minute, letting the pride she felt in her effort wash over her.

Lydia sighed again and glanced at the digital alarm clock next to Gene's side of the bed. Four more hours until he would be home. Poking a finger through the strands of her thick brown hair, she touched one of the orange juice cans that she had rolled her waist-length tresses with that morning. She shook her head at the dampness deep inside.

It was too early to fix her hair anyway. Too early to dress. Too early to start looking out the window for Gene's pickup. Still, she nudged the blinds apart in hopes that maybe a car or truck would pass down the gravel road that ran in front of the trailer.

Lydia didn't mind the isolation of their trailer and had, in the beginning, been proud of the way Gene refused to live in a trailer court.

"I don't want my wife surrounded by no trailer trash," he'd boasted when her mother questioned the soundness of living ten miles from the nearest neighbor. "And besides," he'd add when her mother pushed the issue, "if people keep moving to Clara City and Kingsport, this land'll be worth ten times what I paid for it in a few years." That had been five years ago.

Lydia hadn't seen any evidence of the urban sprawl Gene was sure would come. She sat gingerly on the edge of the king-sized waterbed and ran her fingers along the hem of her dressiest dress, polyester jade green that fit her like a second skin. She knew she looked hot in it. Fingering the ruffles that framed the low-cut collar, Lydia wished she could have taped her favorite soaps.

That would have been pushing it though. Gene didn't often check to make sure she hadn't taped an unapproved show, but she wasn't willing to take that chance; it would only spoil tonight. Oh, he let her tape her shows on occasion. If she had a good excuse. And she used that yesterday. Boy, *that* was close, she thought. But it wasn't my fault. Who ever heard of a florist not having roses?

Lydia had driven into Clara City, with Gene's permission, to get groceries. Thursday wasn't her usual day to go the store, but she had told him that she wanted to make a banana pudding and needed fresh bananas. That was all of the surprise she was willing to let on about; she was making his favorite dessert for Friday night.

She had walked the six blocks to the florist so that Gene wouldn't be able to tell that she had gone even a tenth of a mile out of her way. When Mr. Williams had told her he had used the last of the roses for Larry Peters' casket spray, Lydia's determination exceeded her disappointment. Nothing was going to spoil their fifth anniversary celebration. Nothing. She knew, deep down, that Gene was planning a special surprise too, and she didn't want him to think that she hadn't tried to make it a night to remember.

All the way back to the car she had argued with herself. Should she drive the extra twenty-five miles to Kingsport to get the rose petals or not?

Gene would get upset when he discovered that there were fifty more miles on the odometer than there should have been. Would it matter if she didn't have them? It would to her. How would she ify the unexplained trip? She could say that her grandmother had taken ill and went to visit. Why hadn't she called the shop to ask permission? The nursing home had called at noon and she didn't want to disturb him at lunch. He knew that she knew never, ever to bother him on his lunch break. If she didn't leave right away, she wouldn't have been home when he arrived. He got really mad if she wasn't home when he arrived.

"No. No. No," she said, "don't think bad thoughts." As soon as she felt the gentle swaying of the bed, she jumped back up. She didn't want the waves to disturb the rose petals it had taken her almost an hour to carefully place between the crisp white cotton sheets.

Lydia clasped her hands in front of her and walked around the edge of the bed. She stopped and ran a blunt-nailed finger along the buttonhole of Gene's blue-pinstriped suit that she had pressed and laid out that morning. "I should have saved a rose for his lapel," she muttered. "I'm so stupid." Her voice rose and echoed in the room. Why didn't I think of that?" Her voice dropped to almost a whisper, the words running together in one long sentence. "I'm so selfish. What'll I do?" Lydia's eyes darted around the room.

"Stop it!" she told herself loudly and firmly. "You never think, that's your problem." That was what Gene was always telling her: you never think. "Now stop and think." Lydia forced her trembling hands to her side. "Think!" As she stood there, pressing her breath into short, regulated spasms, her mind remained blank. As her heart began to slow, thoughts began to form. It doesn't have to be a rose. Any flower will do. He won't know about the roses until we get in bed and then---

Lydia knew how disinterested in anything else Gene was when he was aroused. All he would be able to think of was getting his dick in her pussy. He wouldn't even notice the rose petals; but she would. Maybe tonight, if she did everything right, he would caress her and fondle her, not rub his hand on her pussy three times before shifting his weight toward her. Tonight, she would lie among the petals and he wouldn't get upset if she stroked his back while he moved on top of her. Maybe tonight, he would kiss her while he was inside of her. Maybe tonight, he would...

Shaking her head to dislodge the fantasy, Lydia looked around the room. She was calmer now, but she felt the dampness between her legs. Maybe tonight ... Spying the plastic-flowered centerpiece on the coffee table, she borrowed one of the large orange and yellow flowers, whose name she didn't know, and trotted back to the bedroom, smiling, to place it in the buttonhole.

Six hours later, Lydia stood at the kitchen counter and tossed the salad again, trying to keep it from getting too soggy. Gene hated soggy salad. "I should have waited to add the dressing," she muttered. "I'm so stupid."

She looked at the clock on the stove while she tossed. She had expected him to be a little late, but not this late. "Something to do with the surprise, I'm sure," she kept murmuring as she tried not to worry. Gene hated for her to worry. So she didn't. Not out loud anyway. "He's okay. He got hung up. And he probably had to work some overtime." Gene often had to work overtime, especially on Friday nights. Lydia put the bowl back in the refrigerator, smoothed her skirt and went back into the bedroom to add some more cologne.

Finally she heard his truck pull into the driveway. She listened at the door as the truck door slammed, the grinding of his boots on the gravel and the opening and shutting of her old Rambler. When she heard his boot hit the bottom of the metal stairs, Lydia scurried into the kitchen, quickly tying her mother's company's-coming apron around her waist. She pushed her curled hair over her shoulders, placed her left hand on the stove and flashed her best smile.

"Hey there handsome," she sang out as Gene burst through the door. Her smile quickly faded as her eyes searched his arms for the bouquet of flowers she had been sure he would have stopped to buy. Her eyes welled up as she met storm clouds in his eyes. Gene tromped across the small vestibule and into the kitchen. Lydia could smell the beer as he grabbed her by the chin, his fingers digging into the empty sockets along her jaw.

"Where'd ya go?" He shook her chin; her hair flew about her shoulders.

Lydia couldn't reply.

"Where'd ya go?" His fingers gouged deeper.

"Gr-r-an-d-ma gggot sick."

"That old bag is always sick. Didn't I tell you to stay the fuck away from there?"

"BBBut she---"

Gene released his grip on her chin. Noticing the green dress, the white frilly apron, the black spiked heels, he grabbed her arm. "Whatta you all fucking gussied up for?"

"I, ah, I---"

"Think I'm gonna take you out?" He pushed her across the room. "I wouldn't go anywhere with a fat cow like you."

"I mmmade your favorite dinner." Her hands shook as she gestured helplessly toward the kitchen, then the table.

Gene pulled the oven door open and peered inside. "It's fucking burnt."

Lydia ran over to the oven door. "Oh, no. No. Cheese always gets black like that when it's cooked."

Lydia stumbled from the backhand across her cheek. Her stocking caught on the oven door, ripping a big hole mid-calf.

"Don't argue with me, goddamn you."

Lydia's eyes rooted to the steel-toes of Gene's work boots. "I-I-I---" Lydia stammered "I, ah, I made lasagna and salad and, and banana pudding. Your favorite." She smiled but there wasn't much effort in it.

Gene took two lurching steps and yanked open the refrigerator door. "Where's the goddamned beer?"

"I, ah, I didn't put any in." Lydia lifted her head and tried to smile. "I chilled some wine."

"Wine's for fucking fags and women." Gene put his face directly in front of Lydia's. Beer-and-cigarette breath rushed up her nose. "You think I'm a fag?"

No reply.

"You think I'm a fucking fag?"

Gene drew back his hand.

"NO!" Lydia was vehement in her denial.

Gene grabbed Lydia by the hair, her knees buckling as her head wrenched backward. "Get them clothes off. I'll show you how a man fucks."

"BBBUt dinn---"

He pulled her head further back. "I said get them goddamn clothes off; I wanna fuck." He thrust his free hand down the front of her dress, grabbed her nipple and squeezed. Lydia sucked in her breath. He released his grip and shoved her toward the bedroom. "Hurry up."

Lydia scampered toward the bedroom, untying the apron as she brushed past him.

***

Gene awoke with the sun shining in his eyes, his head throbbing from tying one on last night. Groaning, he made his way to the bathroom, took a leak, and stumbled into the kitchen.

Lydia sat at the tiny table, eyes on the Formica, still in her faded cotton nightgown. Her face was covered with purple and black bruises, dried blood scabbed on her upper lip, and her left eye almost swollen shut.

Gene grimaced when he looked at her. He got a drink of water from the tap and tiptoed over to Lydia. "Lyddie, I'm so sorry," he whispered. "Why do you make me do this to you? All you had to do was remind me it was our anniversary and I woulda stopped and gotten you that new skillet you been pestering me about."

Lydia flinched at the sound of his voice.

"Why don't you think? I wouldn't have to do this if you would think."

Lydia flinched again as Gene began to stroke her tangled hair.

"We'll go for a ride today. Would you like that? Maybe even stop for lunch? How 'bout it?" He nestled her neck. "You forgive your ol' Dreamy Geney?"

***

"I found it lying next to the thing where you put the buggies at the grocery store," Lydia told Gene as he examined the navy blue leather purse she had found lying in Super Saver's parking lot. "Nobody else was around—I parked away from the other cars like you always tell me to--- and I would have been late if I had taken it in to the manager, and I, ah, I thought I could drop it off at the owner's house tomorrow." She looked up at Gene. "If you don't mind, that is."

He pulled out the matching wallet. "Find any money?"

"I didn't even look inside; I was waiting for you," Lydia lied.

Gene didn't comment as he rummaged through the credit card slots, the pictures of two kids in various stages of development, and the change compartment. He took the coins and spread them in his callused palm. "Forty-five fucking cents," he muttered, putting the coins in the pocket of his work shirt. Lying the wallet on the table, he dumped the purses' other contents on the table. A small calendar, a checkbook whose cover matched the purse, a tube of lipstick, a brush, some change and four grocery coupons. He picked up the penny and the quarter and added them to the collection in his pocket.

"I bet the owner really needs this," Lydia said as she picked up the calendar and began to look through it. Gene grunted as she read off today's appointments. "Nine-fifteen haircut; noon, lunch with Susie, three o'clock soccer practice---Charlie; six thirty softball game—Amber; eight o'clock dinner with the Colby's at the Club." She looked up Gene and sighed. "I can't wait to have kids."

"It's not my fucking fault you're not knocked up yet."

Lydia looked down at the floor and shrugged. At first, she had been thrilled that Gene wanted to knock her up as soon as possible. As they settled into married life, she worried how a baby might upset him, especially if it was a colicky one. Still, every month she was disappointed when the red stain appeared on her panties; a baby would give her something to do besides clean the trailer and go to the grocery store. She picked up the checkbook, opened it and let out a long, low whistle.

Gene's head snapped up.

"This belongs to Madeleine and Leon Wolffe."

"Never heard of 'em." Gene shifted his attention back to the credit cards.

Me neither, but listen to this address. 77 Widaman Lane, Kingsport, Arkansas."

Gene reached over and jerked the small rectangle out of her hand. Widaman Lane was in Borough Estates, where the old cotton money lived. "This oughta be worth fucking something," he said as he flapped the checkbook in front of Lydia's face, hitting her nose.

Lydia didn't reply and watched him pace the length of the trailer.

"This oughta be worth fucking something. Okay. Here's what ya do. Tomorrow you, no tonight, tonight I'll call, shit that's long distance, doesn't matter, I'll probably get a couple of hundred out of this, I'll---"

"Huh? How do you figure that--"

Turning, Gene strode back to the table and knocked Lydia upside the head. "A goddamn reward, you stupid bitch, don't you ever think? I want a reward for not using these fucking credit cards!"

"Oh."

"So, here's the plan. I call the bitch tonight and tell her I found her purse and you'll take it over to her house tomorrow. I'd do it myself, but I can't get off work and I know that she'll be *fucking grateful* to get it back." He grabbed the checkbook from the table and headed for the phone in the bedroom.

Lydia smiled, then winced as the cut beneath her lower lip widened. She carefully wiped the tiny droplets of blood away with the back of her hand. Most of the bruises from last week's anniversary celebration had almost faded, but the cut was stubborn in healing. She waited while he punched in the number before looking at the flour canister where the thousand dollars she had taken out of the wallet was hiding.

"Hello, may I speak to Mrs. Wolffe please," Gene said. "I'm sorry to disturb you but---" He could be a charmer when he wanted something. "In Super Saver's parking lot." Lydia listened as he made the arrangements. Ten o'clock tomorrow morning. No, no, isn't any trouble at all. My wife will bring it by; I have to work. Happy to be of service. Yes, I'm sure you're *grateful*."

"Now remember," Gene said as he came out of the bedroom, "you get fucking something for this."

Lydia didn't reply.

Gene grabbed her by the arm, pulling her out of the chair. "Understand?"

Lydia nodded.

"Don't fuck it up either." Gene pushed her toward the kitchen. "Now, fix something for dinner."

Lydia reached for the cast iron skillet beneath the oven and began to prepare to fry the chicken she had taken out of the freezer this morning.

***

The next morning, Lydia stood naked in the bathroom. She shook her head and leaned away from the mirror. She tilted her head. First, left. Then right. She added a few more dabs of concealing makeup to the jaundiced patch beneath her left eye and to the greenish fingerprints around her chin. The bruises were fading, but they were still noticeable if she didn't wear makeup.

She smiled tentatively as she surveyed her handiwork, causing the cut to widen again. She leaned back over the sink to apply another coat of dark red lipstick. Straightening, she pulled her hair back. "It'll do," she said picking up Madeleine's driver's license and holding it up next to the mirror. Lydia's face was much rounder than Madeleine's and her hair was darker and longer. "Okay, so I gained a few pounds and let my hair grow out. Roots and all."

The anniversary celebration had been her lucky night after all. If Gene hadn't hit her, she would have had to go to Clara City to do her shopping. He hated for her to show up in Clara City with her stupidity blazing from her face. "I get fucking tired of explaining to people how I'm training you to fucking think," he'd told her six months after their marriage, "Go to fucking Kingsport when I tell you to get something."

Lydia left for 77 Widaman Lane a half-hour early. She didn't want to be late. She knew where the subdivision was, but had never crossed through the wrought iron gate.

She drove slowly along the winding road, gazing wondrously at the mansions that lined the road. Every one became her favorite. When she came to a dead end, she realized that she had forgotten to read the street signs as she inched by. "You're so stupid," she told herself as she turned the car around.

The second intersection was marked "Widaman Lane." She turned left and looked closely at the house numbers 55, 59, 63. The houses here were even bigger than the ones she had passed. Lydia pulled around the cul-de-sac. A boy and a girl were playing Frisbee on the manicured lawn of number seventy-seven.

Lydia slowed, watching them through the passenger window, then the rear view mirror. She started to make the turn again when the front door of the Georgian-style house flew open and a woman about Lydia's size, a hundred and fifty pounds ago, called something to the children. Lydia stopped the car, turning to watch woman disappear behind the double doors and the children resume their game.

***

"What do you mean she 'wasn't home'?" Gene stormed when she told him that she still had the purse. "She said she'd be there!"

"She wasn't home," Lydia lied. "I didn't want to leave it lying in front of the door. Then I might not get the reward if I didn't hand it to her myself."

Gene stopped and thought. "Fucking a," he said slowly. "See? You can think when you want to. Now fix me some dinner." He slapped her playfully on the butt as she passed. "Fucking good, babe."

As Lydia fixed the chicken fried steak and mashed potatoes she went over the plan in her mind. It had formed quickly as she'd watched the children playing.

She would go back to the trailer, call Madeleine and tell her that her grandmother in Clara City was sick and that she would bring the purse tomorrow. When she would offer to come and get it, she'd say, "No. No. It's no trouble. Grandma has these bouts all the time, and I need to go check on her. Tomorrow morning, ten o'clock again? Good. See you then."

Tomorrow she would leave an hour early, park the car inside the gates, then stroll casually down the sidewalk, the navy blue purse dangling from her shoulder. She loved seeing the flowers blooming in immaculate beds lining the brick homes, the neatly trimmed bushes, the carpets of bright green grass. It was so different from the cotton fields and pastures surrounding the trailer. She would knock at Madeleine's door, graciously enter, then accept a cup of coffee and then tell her how she came to find the purse.

"Well," she would say, "It was a little after three, and I had stopped at Super Saver's to get some bread. When I was putting my buggy away---don't you hate people who leave their buggy in the middle of the lot? ---I saw it lying on the ground. Since I was running late—I always try to be home when my husband gets home, I'm sure you do the same---I didn't have time to run it in to the manager. I didn't touch a thing. As a matter of fact, I'd even forgotten about it until Gene and I were having coffee after dinner. We looked through it together, hoping there'd be some a license or something."

Then she would wait as Madeleine looked through the purse. "No, there wasn't any money in it," she would say and smile sweetly. "When Gene and I looked for some identification, all we found is what's there. We got your phone number from the checkbook. Somebody must have gotten there before me. I'm sorry. At least the bandit didn't take your credit cards and checks."

Madeleine would agree and offer her another cup of coffee. She would refuse, saying she had a busy day and had to get home. Then Madeleine would offer her a reward. "No, No," she would say. "I don't want any reward. It's the only civilized thing to do." Then Madeleine would insist. "Well, if you insist," she'd say sweetly. "I'll put it in church next Sunday."

***

Lydia left the trailer an hour early the next morning and parked outside the gates, walked along Country Club Lane, and pretended that she lived in the Tudor mansion on the corner. She whistled happily as she strolled down the smooth sidewalk, even waving to the two cars that passed her. At ten minutes to ten she went back to her car and headed for the cul-de-sac. But when she rounded the corner, she saw Madeleine sitting on the porch step, watching the children romp with a cocker spaniel.

Lydia slowed and waved. Madeleine waved a small wave back. Lydia completed the circle and stopped in the same spot she had yesterday. She watched for a few minutes before getting out of the car and walking toward Madeleine.

As she had walked shyly up the sidewalk, Madeleine stood and stared at her. Up close, Lydia could see that the two didn't look anything alike. Madeleine's face was much more pointed, her eyes were a deeper brown than Lydia's, her nose was more pugged, and she was, in fact, several inches shorter than Lydia.

"Mrs. Wolffe?"

Madeleine nodded a barely perceptible nod.

Lydia handed her the purse. She wasn't invited in; she wasn't offered a cup of coffee. She wasn't even asked her name.

Madeleine opened it, pulling out the wallet and opening it. "I knew it would be gone. Leon is going to kill me."

"Well, I, ah, there wasn't any money. I swear."

Madeleine continued to flip through the wallet. The credits cards were all there and so were the kids' pictures.

"I swear there wasn't any money in it. Somebody must have gotten there before me. I swear ther---"

Madeleine lifted a slightly trembling hand. "No, no, I didn't mean to imply that. It's that there was--- I had a, a, a lot of cash on me."

Lydia shook her head knowingly. She didn't have to be smart to figure out what Gene would do to her if she lost that kind of money. "But you got your credit cards back," she said sympathetically. "That could have been worse. A lot worse."

Madeleine took a deep breath. "Yes, you're right. I should thank my lucky stars that all they took was the money. Leon would get terribly upset if--- Well, you're kind to bring it all this way."

Lydia blushed. "No problem. We knew that you would be *grateful* to get them back."

"I am. Thank you." Madeleine stared at Lydia.

Lydia shifted her weight.

"Oh. Oh. I, ah, I, don't have any cash on me. I could write you a check?"

"Heavens to Betsy! I didn't mean that. I meant that you would be relieved." She wanted to ask for a tour of the house, but the words hung in her throat.

Madeleine nodded her head. "Yes, I am. Thank you much."

Lydia smiled. "You're welcome. Well, I guess I'll go now," she said as she turned away.

***

Fifty fucking dollars!" Gene stormed through the trailer that night. "That bitch's worth millions and she only gave you fifty dollars?" He swept the five ten-dollar bills off the table, knocking Lydia's hands from beneath her chin at the same time.

She tried to make herself smaller in the chair. Lydia smiled weakly. "Well, I-I-I reminded her that there was lots of credit cards and that nothing else was missing," she lied. It took all her will power not to look toward the sofa where she had hidden Madeleine's driver's license and the remaining nine hundred and fifty dollars.

Gene mimicked her in a high pitched voice. "I reminded her that the credit cards were still there. I can't fucking believe it! You should have said that you were sure there would be a reward. You don't **ever** fucking think, do you, Lyddie? Fifty lousy---" he threw himself into his recliner and reared back. "Fucking dollars."

Lydia went into the kitchen to fix dinner. It would be better if she didn't say much right now; give Gene a chance to calm down.

As he was gnawing the last pork chop bone, she finally asked in a low voice, "Can I go to Kingsport tomorrow? There's a sale at Rupert's. You need a new work shirt."

***

Lydia left the trailer that morning, driving straight to Borough Estates. She'd think of what to tell Gene later. She parked the car inside the wrought iron gate and began to saunter through the subdivision. She was wearing her dressiest dress, the low-heeled pumps she got on sale at Wal-

Mart last summer, a black purse hanging from her shoulder with only Madeleine's driver's license and the money inside.

As she walked, Lydia pretended she was Madeleine Wolffe.

I'm Madeleine. Madeleine Wolffe, she'd say to any neighbor she happened to meet. I live down the street. On Widaman Lane. Surely you've seen my husband and my two kids playing touch football in the front yard.

The funniest thing happened yesterday. Our cocker spaniel, Dandies, got out of the yard and ran lickety-split down the street with Leon and children chasing him. It was the funniest thing. I haven't seen Leon run like that since he played high school football.

Dandies managed to cut a path through the poor man who lives on the corner's tulips. Not to worry though. My gardener, Lester, will repair the damage. Lester is a whiz with flowers. He's expensive, but for a beautiful garden, Leon and I don't care what we pay.

When Lydia reached the turn for Widaman Lane, she halted. Should she? Maybe.

Madeleine would be setting on the stoop again. Should she risk it? Why not? She hadn't seen another living soul all morning.

Lydia walked to where she had parked the car the day before. She glanced up the street and let out a breath she didn't know she was holding. No one was in front of 77 Widaman Lane. She strutted along the sidewalk to the Wolffe residence. She sat on the stoop for a moment, then ran her hand along the bevel-glassed front door and the brass knocker. Peering inside, she could see a huge chandelier reflected in the marbled floor of the wide entryway. A grandfather clock, inside the door, rang twelve times, its peals sending shivers down Lydia's spine.

Lydia wrenched herself away from the cool glass. She'd better go if she was going to get everything done and get home before Gene.

Lydia drove straight through Kingsport and another thirty miles to Salisbury. She still hadn't thought of what she would tell Gene, but she had the drive back to come up with something.

When she arrived in Salisbury, she parked in front of the Farmer's Bank and went inside. "I would like to open a checking account," she said in a low voice to the receptionist.

"Your name?"

"Wolffe." Lydia could hear her voice shaking. "Madeleine Wolffe." What if they knew the Wolffe's here, Lydia wondered. I hadn't thought of that.

"If you'll have a seat, someone will be with in a moment." The receptionist pointed to the gray cushioned chairs.

Lydia held her breath as she watched the bank clerk take out the forms and ask for her driver's license. "Rotten picture, isn't it," she said as she handed Madeleine's license to the woman.

"They always are. You should see mine. How much did you want to deposit this morning?"

Lydia squirmed in the chair. She spent the next thirty minutes opening the account and picking out the checks—it was a tough choice, daffodil yellow or sky blue; she finally chose daffodil yellow. "Oh, by the way," she said, "Could you send the statement to my sister's house? Rt. 6, Box 5736. I'm saving up to take my husband on an Alaskan cruise for our anniversary next year, and I want it to be a *total* surprise." Lydia smiled sweetly and reached out to the touch the clerk on the arm. "It'll be between us."

The clerk nodded in conspiracy and went to process Lydia/Madeleine's application.

Outside, Lydia took a deep breath. She had enough time to drive by Madeleine's again before she had to be home. And she still had to think of something to tell Gene about the extra mileage.

***

The next day, she took the checkbook out of its hiding place---in the Kotex box beneath the bathroom sink---and waited a full hour after Gene left before heading for Kingsport. She drove slowly, the yellow line barely visible in the peripheral of her right eye; the left was swollen shut. Gene didn't think much of her for going to Salisbury to get him new work pants that were on sale five dollars cheaper than in Kingsport.

When she reached Borough Estates, she drove to the edge of the cul-de-sac and waited. She only had to wait a minute before the kids bounded out the door, school backpacks dangling from their hands. Lydia smiled as they piled into the van. She imagined them arguing over who was going to ride shotgun. The doorway framed Madeleine and Leon as they embraced and kissed. Lydia looked away from the tender moment, touching her swollen eye. Madeleine waved as the van backed out of the drive, then retreated back into the house. Lydia waved too as the van passed her. Leon waved back.

Lydia waited several minutes, long enough for the van to get out of the subdivision, before re-starting the engine. The car idled at the intersection, its blinker beckoning her toward the trailer. Instead, she turned and headed for the Salisbury Mall.

She spent the rest of the morning and the early afternoon opening charge accounts at Penney's, Sears, Montgomery Ward, Irma Dumas, and Singleton's. No one looked closely at the driver's license she handed them; no one questioned she her status as housewife.

For the next month, Lydia left the trailer every morning to watch Madeleine send her children off to school and her husband off to work, making sure she was back at the trailer before the mail arrived. As each of the credit cards were delivered, Lydia placed them in their hiding place beneath the bathroom sink.

After all the cards had been safely stored away, Lydia began to wait outside the Wolffe's home for longer and longer periods of time. She loved to watch the kid's head off for school. She was worried that Madeleine would notice her, but she seemed wrapped up in her own little happy world.

After the kids were gone, Lydia would shop for awhile, charging scarves, hats, jewelry, blouses, dresses, trinkets to her new self. No one questioned her; no one asked for identification. Most of the items she would return the following afternoon, afraid to let Gene find them in the trailer.

***

At two-thirty, she hurried back to Widaman Lane and watched as the Wolffe children bounded off the school bus. Lydia imagined them going in to plates of homemade chocolate chip cookies and fresh cold milk. She slid down in the seat, hoping they would come out to play.

Several songs played low on the radio when the door to 77 Widaman Lane finally opened. Madeleine came out, her face swollen in various shades of purple, black, and blue, and headed for the mailbox at the end of the driveway.

Lydia sat straight up and thrust her head over the steering wheel. She's had an accident, she thought. Lydia pushed open the car door and jumped out.

"Madeleine! Madeleine!"

Madeleine turned.

"What happened? Are you all right?" Lydia's voice was frantic.

"Who are you?"

Lydia stopped. She had forgotten that Madeleine didn't know who she was.

Madeleine repeated her question.

"I, ah, I'm the woman who found your purse about two months ago."

Madeleine stared at the woman in the cheap polyester slacks and sweatshirt. "Oh yes. Thank you again."

"What happened? Were you in a car accident? Are the kids all right?"

Madeleine began to back away from Lydia.

Lydia grabbed her arm.

"What happened?"

"I fell down. That's all. I fell down. Please. Please leave me alone."

Madeleine turned and ran back into the house.

Lydia started after her, then stopped. She touched the fading purple along her own cheekbone. Nobody got bruises like that from falling down. Even she knew better than to use a lame excuse like that.

She walked slowly back to the car. She sat there for a long time, staring at the beautiful brick mansion with its carpet of green grass, its shiny brass knocker, and the impatiens climbing over themselves as if in a contest to show the brightest colors. She watched as Leon pulled the van in the drive.

After he closed the beautiful oak door with the beveled glass, Lydia took Madeleine's driver's license, the checkbook from Farmer's Bank, and the five credit cards out of her purse. She walked up to the mailbox and gently laid them inside.

I gotta hurry, she thought, Gene'll be home soon.

Credits

Death in the Afternoon
*as "The Death of Me Yet," *Gigantic,* University of Missouri-St. Louis, 1998.
*as a one-act play *Stirring: A Literary Collection,* 2000.
Taj Mahal Review, Vol. 4, No. 1, 2005.

The Fountain of Youth
* *Palimpsest*, Vol. 1, No 1, New Mexico, 2000.

Heart Hunter
Watermark, University of Missouri-St. Louis, 1997.

Sometimes You're the Bug; Sometimes You're the Windshield
*Performed as part of the St. Louis Community College-Forest Park Production, "Let Our Words be Heard and Scene," 1997
* *Steps Astray,* University of Missouri-St. Louis, 1994.

About the Author

Julie Failla Earhart is an internationally published author, most notably in India (seven stories) and the UK. Her work has been also been published in *Cuivre River Anthology, Sweetgum Notes 2.2, Echoes of the Ozarks, The Storyteller; Well- Versed* (2003, 2004 & 2005); *Stirrings: A Literary Collection; Palimpsest* (inaugural issue); *Gigantic; Watermark; Words and Dreams, Part XII; An Archer's Dream*; and *Steps Astray*. She is still working on an as-yet-untitled second collection. She obtained her bachelor's degree and her Master of Fine Arts degree from the University of Missouri-St. Louis. She abandoned academic teaching and freelancing for a steady, full-time job (with free health insurance) in the Marketing Dept. of the St. Louis Public Library. Her success continues in the nonfiction world, where she still writes for *Sauce Magazine, Armchair Interviews E-zine* and *Show-Me Missouri* magazine. Julie maintains her creative writing classes with Chesterfield Arts and St. Louis Writer's Workshop. She lives in St. Louis, Missouri.

Note: Julie is under no illusion that the stories in this collection represent her writing abilities. The stories printed in this collection represent the work she created during her undergraduate years at UM-SL. She realizes that they will never be picked up by a literary journal in their current condition but is tired of working them. They were written between 1994 and 2000. Julie self-published them so her nephew Joseph would have something to remember her by when he gets older and, hopefully, will appreciate her talents and wonder about goofy ol' Aunt Julie.

www.ingramcontent.com/pod-product-compliance
Lightning Source LLC
Chambersburg PA
CBHW031840170626
46807CB00004B/1556